BOOKS BY CHRIS'
MYERS/CLARISSA

CW00704866

THE ALEDAN S
PSION MATES P
The Aledan PSIO⌐
OLTARIN
SURVIVING ZEVUS MAR
PSION FACTOR
PSION'S CHILDREN
CALAN

CYBORG AWAKENING SERIES
CYBORG AWAKENINGS Prequel
VYKEN DARK

WITH CLARISSA LAKE
JOLT SOMBER
TALIA'S CYBORG
AXEL REX

CYBORG RANGER SERIES
BLAZE
DARKEN
STALKER
MAX

MAX
Cyborg Ranger

Clarissa Lake
Christine Myer

ISBN: 9798352085790
ASIN: B0BCZTT9SQ

Contains Sexually Explicit Scenes

CONTENTS

Chapter One

Max Steele glided his hybrid hover cycle flyer to a stop on a mountain peak. Gazing over the snow-covered mountains, the ancient Blue Mountain Observatory drew his attention. The old observatory should have been preserved as a monument to humankind's quest to understand the stars. Instead, it stood in ruin from centuries of neglect.

After months of getting to know his assigned territory and its people, his orders had changed. They were moving him to northern California to command a unit of a hundred protectors.

His weekly reports had talked him out of his current job. The farmers and ranchers in his territory, comprised of Montana, Wyoming, and Idaho, were a self-sufficient breed. They did not need an elite cyborg ranger to restore law and order because they had maintained it even after the Mesaarkans bombed every major city on Earth. The whole region only had a population of a few small cities, so the Mesaarkans passed over those states in favor of heavier population centers.

Max had treasured the quiet moments of solitude in places like this, and he only had to deal with people in small doses. He was a cyborg who didn't have the best people skills. His marine ranger team was his family. He didn't really mind unenhanced humans, but he felt awkward relating to them personally. He preferred his own company to socializing with any but his cyborg brothers.

This lightly populated area was perfect for him to oversee. But he had to admit he wasn't truly needed here. These people were used to fending for themselves before the war began. His training as a field medic was required more often than law enforcement. It had often been the same in the war. Max was a formidable warrior as well.

He thought he was doing well in his solitary life on Phantom, working in cyber-tech repair and replacement. Max did feel a yearning to find his genetic mate, but the prospect also worried him. He had a hard time sharing his emotions with his friends. What if he couldn't give his female the emotional support she needed? Her avatar had even lamented he was too closed off. What would his real mate think?

There was no sense in worrying about what might never happen. The avatar wasn't real; she was a projection based on his mate's genetic profile. Perhaps he would have a better outcome once exposed to her pheromones.

Stalker assured him there were beautiful mountains in California, too. He just needed to pick a spot where his prefab dwelling could be set up. Meanwhile, Max could sleep almost anywhere. His ranger team had often slept on the bare ground during the war; and he could do so again if necessary.

With a rueful sigh, he restarted the sky cycle and morphed it into flyer mode to head west to California. Stalker had suggested some areas to scout for setting up his house within a hundred-mile radius of the megalopolis of San Francisco.

A few hours later, he was gliding over mountains and farmland searching for a potential location where he might set up his home without close neighbors. He took snapshots of a few promising sites through his ocular camera, storing them along with their coordinates on his internal computer.

Falyn Wayne cantered her horse Angus along the crumbling pavement on her way home from town. The dark bay gelding had a smooth canter he could maintain for long distances, and Falyn took great pleasure in riding him. He had been her only means of transportation besides her two feet for almost nine years.

Lost in her thoughts about the chores she had to finish when she returned to her homestead, Falyn didn't hear the hoofbeats fast approaching behind her. When the sound broke through her inner musings, she looked behind her and saw four riders racing toward her at full gallop. A shiver of fear rippled through her.

Falyn rarely saw one rider on this road leading to her small farm but four riders racing toward her could only be trouble. She must be their target at the speed they were coming after her. "Angus, run!" she kicked his sides and urged him forward with her hands.

Angus responded immediately as if he was born to run. He was fast and powerful, and easily increased the distance between them and the riders following them. Attempting to avoid leading them straight to her home, Falyn steered Angus off the road onto an old game trail that was actually a shortcut. The low hanging branches meant they had to move slower but they were familiar with those paths, and it would be faster through the wooded area. Soon they emerged into a great meadow stretching ahead for acres.

Once in the open field, Angus lengthened his stride into a full gallop across the open ground; he knew the path home.... Falyn hoped the other riders missed the game trail and she'd lost them. She started to believe they were going to make it home, until Angus, stumbled and crashed to the ground with a painful scream.

Falyn went sailing through the air and hit the grass rolling. The impact knocked the wind out of her, and she briefly lost consciousness.

Stunned and disoriented, it took her two tries to push to her hands and knees as she heard her horse's painful whinny. She scanned the ground around her and found her beautiful horse lying on his side.

"Oh no, Angus!" Falyn pushed herself to her feet and stumbled toward him. She saw the problem immediately as she looked him over. His front leg had a bend where it shouldn't be.

She walked over to him; she fell to her knees by his head, weeping softly. "I am so sorry, Angus," she sobbed, stroking his great head.

The horse tried to roll onto his belly to get up and whinnied in pain. "No, baby. Don't try to get up. It will only hurt more." Falyn choked on a sob as she stood, knowing what she had to do. There was no fixing his broken leg.

Nine years, only nine years since she found him in her front yard one day. He was a spindly-legged colt all alone. She didn't know where he came from or how he got there but she took him in. He was only nine years old, not that old for a horse.

He was in pain and suffering from an injury she couldn't fix. He would die a long slow death or be eaten alive by mountain lions. Still crying softly, Falyn stood and pulled out the pistol from the holster at her right hip. Holding it pointed at the horse's head in both hands. Tears blinded her, but she couldn't make her trigger finger move.

Wiping her face on her muslin shirt sleeve, she pointed the gun at the horse's head again, but her hands were shaking. How could she just kill him?

A memory flashed of him as a colt following her everywhere on the property as she went about her daily chores. One day he had even followed her into the kitchen. Her hands still shook as she tried to point the gun.

Flying over a valley, Max spotted a lone horseback rider fleeing from a group of riders a quarter mile behind. Max had no way to tell who was a victim or perpetrator, but the lone rider, a female, was clearly disadvantaged.

Calculating where best to set down, he lowered his vehicle to the ground in a vertical landing in front of the group. Pulling his ion rifle from the sling under his leg, he jumped off and pointed it at the oncoming horsemen.

The four reined their horses to a halt twenty feet before him.

"Just stop right there, gentlemen," he commanded. "Don't even think of pulling those side arms. You will all be dead before you get a shot off."

"Who the fuck are you?"

"Law enforcement Ranger Max Steele, here to protect and serve. Why are you chasing the female?"

"She escaped, and we are trying to bring her back," said the dark-haired bearded man.

"Since she was running away, I don't think she wants to return. That makes me think I need to protect her freedom."

"She stole that horse from the boss. We were trying to get it back."

"Oh, but you said you were trying to take *her* back."

"Because she stole the horse..." the leader insisted.

Max frowned as he assessed each man. He was tempted to just kill them for lying. An ordinary human might have believed the leader, but his heart rate and blood pressure spike gave him away. More likely, they were some overlord's thugs, and she either escaped the harem or they were traffickers.

"Who does the horse belong to?"

"Our boss, Thorne Driscoll."

"Describe it."

The apparent leader paused with a frown and thought for a moment. "I think it's the big dark bay stud."

"You can't describe the horse, but you know she stole it?"

"I didn't see her take it. The stable hand said it was that one."

"Is there a brand or tattoo that identifies the owner?"

"There should be," the other man hedged.

"I see." Max lowered his rifle from his shoulder but still held it ready. Shooting them would leave a mess to clean up and require explanations. "Well, since I am the law enforcer here, I will go after the female and question her. I will examine the horse and determine who is the rightful owner."

"We have our orders…." The beard protested.

"And I am the law enforcer. You will stand down, or I will put you down."

"You think you can take us all on by yourself?"

"I know I can. Do you know what a cyborg is? I am a cyborg marine ranger. Your ordinary projectile weapons are only an annoyance. I could take you all down before you could do sufficient damage to stop me," Max told them calmly. "You either stand down, or I will make you."

The bearded man eyed Max, and his high-tech rifle casually pointed in their direction. Max waited.

"Have it your way. Let's go, guys." Bearded man turned his horse and urged it into a gallop, with his cronies following suit.

Max ran back to his cycle. Stowing his rifle in its sling, he jumped on and set off after the lone female. He found her sooner than expected, half a mile away.

Her horse lay on the ground, and she stood over it, holding a pistol pointed at its head in both hands, sobbing.

Max dropped his hovering craft to the ground with a thud and leaped off, running. "Wait! Don't shoot!" he yelled.

Startled, the female whirled and pointed her pistol at him, her face streaked with tears. "Don't come any closer!"

Max stopped, stunned, not by the gun pointed at him but by her scent. He put up his hands immediately. "Don't shoot. I'm here to help," he assured her in a deceivingly calm tone. Max was anything but.

This female was his genetic mate! How could this be? The first female he met in California, a place he didn't really want to be.

He glanced at the horse and saw its front leg bent where it shouldn't. Was she crying because the horse failed her or because it was hurt?

"I'm not here to hurt you. I am a law enforcer for this territory." He had a deep, rich, masculine voice fitting for a man of his size and stature.

She hadn't noticed the circled gold star patch on his shirt or hat. "Since when? The only law around here are the gang lords."

"We know. That's why the Federation Enclave sent me. Back east, they call them overlords. They don't know it yet, but that will all change." Max moved closer as he spoke, holding her gaze. He couldn't help thinking she was even more beautiful than the avatar they fed his mind in stasis.

She was tall for a woman, but he stood over six and a half feet, so the top of her head barely reached his shoulder.

"I never heard of it."

"I believe you. Do you know about the war when aliens bombed the cities?" Max took a step closer.

"I heard of it, but that all happened before I was born."

"Yes, but it didn't end until five years ago. All the human worlds paid a terrible price for the misdeeds of a few." He stepped closer.

"Stay back!" she flicked off the safety, leveling the gun muzzle at the middle of his chest. She didn't realize until later; the safety was on when she was trying to shoot Angus.

"Go ahead. Shoot. That won't hurt me. I'm a cyborg warrior."

Max took another step closer. By then, he was only about six feet from her. On the last step,   she   fired…

Chapter Two

Max flinched as the bullet struck him. It stung a little but didn't stop him from moving closer and grabbing the gun from the woman.

She stared at him, stunned and horrified. She looked no more stunned than he felt. His genetic mate had just shot him in the chest, a killing shot for an ordinary man, which he was not.

"Omigod!" she cried as he gripped her upper arms. "I'm sorry," she tried to pull away. "Don't hurt me."

"No. Never!" he vowed.

She looked up at him, new tears sliding down her cheeks. "What are you? You should be on the ground dying!" Tears brimmed over her lids as green and gold eyes searched his handsome face.

"A cybernetically and structurally enhanced human, commonly known as a cyborg." Her cyborg, but he didn't say it because he told himself it might upset her more. After all, she had just shot him.

"What happened to the horse? Those men chasing you said you stole it."

"Only after he was stolen from me. ...And now I have to put him down. He stepped into a hole, I think, and fell. ...Threw me clear."

Max stared at her, not realizing he was rubbing his hands up and down her arms. Her oval face was framed by long, disheveled brown hair. Her hazel green eyes dominated over a straight nose and soft-looking full lips. He was utterly taken by her pretty face and curvy figure.

But the intoxicating scent of her pheromones had made his cock harden as soon as he recognized it. He wanted to tell her she was his, but he couldn't get the words out.

"Please, I have to take care of Angus. I can't let him suffer...."

"You mean to shoot him? No, let me look at his injury. I might be able to save his leg."

"Really? You can do that?" She looked up at him, hopefully.

"It works on humans. Let me get my med-kit." Max jogged back to his bike and pulled a plastic case from his cargo compartment. He hurried back and knelt on the ground beside the horse's front legs.

The horse struggled, apparently trying to get up. His female knelt by its head, petting and talking softly to him. Max took out a hand-held scanner and passed it over the injured leg, assessing the damage as it sent the results directly to the cyborg's internal computer. The cannon bone was fractured and displaced.

He checked his databanks and found that he could use his bone repair regimen to stabilize the leg and heal it. Injecting the necessary med and a pain killer, Max straightened the leg and aligned the two parts together, holding them for a couple minutes for the nanite paste to secure them.

"He should be able to stand in 30 minutes, but he will need 24 hours before he can carry a rider."

"How is that possible?" she asked.

"It's the same technology field medics use to get soldiers on their feet and out of danger."

"Those men chasing you said you stole the horse."

"They lied. I've had Angus since he was a colt. They were after me for no good reason. I just went to town to trade with crafters I know. Millie, the weaver, told me women had disappeared since those thugs came to town."

"I knew he was lying, but not why. I sent them back the way they came." He believed her; she was his mate. Max would investigate further after he got Falyn and her horse home.

"Thank you. You have been very kind. I am Falyn Wayne. I have a homestead about ten miles down the old road."

"I am Federation Ranger Max Steele, assigned here to restore law and order to Northern California."

"All by yourself?"

"The cyborg commander is sending a unit of a hundred trained protectors to help."

"You will need them." Falyn paused to study him, still stroking her horse's head in her lap. He stared at her as if he couldn't take his eyes off her.

Looking back at him, she felt a flutter of sexual awareness between her thighs. He was a big, handsome, sexy male with bulging muscles under his tight khaki shirt... With the bullet hole in the middle of his chest. There was a small ring of blood around the bullet hole, but that was all.

Falyn closed her eyes and shook her head, remembering she'd shot him point blank. "Omigod, I can't believe I shot you. Are you really all right?" She gave him a worried look.

"It stung just a little. I am fine." He plucked at the hole in his shirt and pulled out the bullet embedded in the skin over his steel alloy breast bone. "See?"

"I was scared… didn't realize I was squeezing the trigger until the gun went off. I'm so sorry. I thought you were one of them."

"Except I was not riding a horse…."

"I didn't even register that. I just knew if you got a hold of me, I wouldn't be able to get away…."

"And you were upset because you thought you needed to kill your own horse." Max closed up his med-kit and stood. "Cyborgs don't hurt females. They could be a genetic mate to one of our brothers. I am here to help."

He turned, walking back to his machine.

"Are you leaving?"

"No, just putting away my med-kit. These devices are hard to get on Earth, and I don't want to lose them." He stowed the kit back in the cargo compartment and then returned to sit beside Falyn in the grassy meadow. "I will not leave you out here alone to wait for your horse to recover."

"Thank you," she said, glancing at him. "You are staring at me again. Should I know you? Or do I remind you of someone?"

He seemed to hesitate before he said, "I...I'm attracted to you... You are very beautiful."

Falyn laughed, and Max seemed taken aback.

"Why do you laugh?"

"I'm sorry. It's just that I'm a mess, covered in dust, and I probably smell like a horse. It's very sweet of you to say... And... I feel attracted to you, too," she admitted, glancing at him shyly.

She didn't smell like a horse at all. He smelled deliciously alluring as he moved a little closer to her.

"I'm glad you're staying. I didn't relish sitting with Angus alone in the dark all night."

Max seemed to want to say something more, but he just moved closer and put his arm around her shoulders. If not for Angus's head in her lap, she might have crawled onto Max's lap to see where things went.

Chapter Three

The sun set shortly after Max sat in the grass beside Falyn. That she hadn't pulled away when he put his arm around her encouraged his hope that she would accept him as her cyborg mate. Yet, he couldn't make himself say the words to her.

Being close to her was not helping his now constant erection. But it was getting cooler with the sunset, and his body heat would help keep her warm. If not for the horse's head on her lap, he would pull her into his arms and kiss her. He could almost feel her soft lips against his.

However, it was important to keep the animal calm while the nanites knitted his bone back together.

"Do people around here know that the war is over?" he asked.

"I think so. I heard that the cyborgs were coming back to help fix things. I'm guessing that's why you are here."

"Yeah. I never planned to come back, but my unit commander got a call for help from Vyken Dark asking us to come. He's the head of cyborgs on Earth. I was living on Phantom, our cyborg colony, working my job, just existing day to day. They promised us that if we survived the war, our genetic mates would be on Earth to welcome us when it was over."

"Let me guess. It was a lie."

"It was one way to control us and a strong incentive for us to keep fighting. They kept telling us to 'do it for *her*.' But when the war ended, only the cyborg converts were returned to Earth. The in vitro bred cyborgs were diverted to Phantom for debriefing. That's when we finally learned the truth."

"There are no genetic mates?" Falyn asked.

"Yes, there are, but not the way we were promised. They were supposed to locate and arrange for us to meet them. It never happened. The Enclave is building a database now, but with limited success. The gene pool used to create us came from Earth, but only a fraction of the cyborgs recently awakened, and those returning have found their mates."

"And what about you? How will you find your mate?" she asked.

"Do you have a mate?" Max asked casually.

"No, but I wasn't hinting."

Max hadn't intended to tell her, but her hopeful expression changed his mind. He paused for a breath, then said, "I didn't have a plan until I found you... Falyn, you are my genetic mate." He gave her a wry smile. "I have been told my social skills are poorly developed. Even my avatar mate complained, and she was AI-driven."

"You got those men off my trail, saved Angus when I thought I had to put him down... and you are incredibly sexy." She smiled at him, flirting shamelessly.

"Does that mean you will accept me as your mate?"

"It means I like you so far and want to get better acquainted."

"I really need to kiss you," he said bluntly. Leaning in and cupping her face, he pressed his lips to hers.

Falyn sighed and moved her lips against his, opening to his exploring tongue. He took his time probing and swirling his tongue around hers. Joy blossomed in his soul as he kissed his genetic mate for the first time. That she kissed him back nurtured the hope that she would accept him as her mate.

But he ended the kiss sooner than he wished as his pants had grown painfully tight in the crotch. The scent of her arousal made it even worse.

"Wow, that was nice," she assured him as their lips parted.

"It was," Max agreed. "I would like to do it again, but it makes me want to breed with you."

"Um, yeah, I understand that. I don't think I have ever reacted to a man like my body is right now. Are you wearing some kind of love potion?"

"No, it's just my pheromones… because we are genetic mates. I can hardly believe it. I didn't want to leave Montana when I first got my orders. I just like the solitude of the mountain where I assembled my home."

"You couldn't ask for an alternate assignment?"

"I didn't have a good reason to make such a request. Captain Savage didn't ask what I wanted; he asked if I would come. Besides, my teammate Stalker is fully extended in the Los Angeles megalopolis. The San Francisco version was not as heavily populated, but Stalker couldn't cover both even with help."

"Well, I am sure glad you arrived when you did…. I am so sorry I shot you. I'm not usually so careless with a gun. I don't like them, but I don't feel safe going to town without one."

"I could see how surprised you were when it went off. I knew it was an accident."

"Thank you for understanding. I swear I will be more careful from now on." Falyn fell silent, stroking her horse's head as he nickered. "I think he's feeling better."

As soon as she said that, Angus rolled from his side and stood. "Well, I guess so!" Falyn stood, examining him in the fading light.

Max stood, took a penlight from his pocket, and shined it on its injured leg so Falyn could see it, too. He also ran a scan from his internal computer. "The bone is set, but I think we should wait until daylight to walk him back to your homestead."

"I should probably take off his saddle and let him graze. I don't know how many miles we ran from those men. I don't even know them or why they were chasing me." Falyn worked at unfastening the cinch on her horse's saddle.

"Human trafficking. It's happening everywhere the overlords and gang bosses rule. We believe they are shipping them to off-world slavers."

"So now I have good reason to be afraid to go to town." She pulled Angus's saddle off and set it by a nearby tree on the ground. Taking up a rope attached to the saddle, she took off his bridle and attached a metal clip to his halter, tethering him to the tree with access to the meadow grass. Angus immediately started grazing.

"He needs water." Falyn went to the canvas saddle bags and pulled out a collapsible bucket.

"I saw a stream about two hundred yards west of here," said Max, holding out his hand. "Let me go get some. I see far better than a normal human in the dark. We don't want Angus to step into another hole.

"Thank you, Max." She handed him the bucket. "Angus would try to follow if I go."

"I'll be back in a couple of minutes."

While Max jogged toward the stream, Falyn untied the sleeping bag from her saddle. It was made from a synthetic material compressed in a compact roll that was easy to tie to the back of a saddle. With the setting sun, the ground was becoming damp. She spread it on the grass by the saddle to use it for a headrest.

Max jogged across the meadow toward a stand of trees that marked the stream's bank a short distance away. With his enhanced vision, he could see almost as good at night as in daylight.

He didn't like leaving Falyn alone, but he knew the horse needed water after the long run and trauma. He downloaded the horse care data while he was tending its broken leg. There was a time when such an injury warranted euthanizing the animal.

Max knew Falyn was his genetic mate almost immediately. After his experience with her avatar in stasis, he'd been reluctant to tell his real mate. He worried she would reject him. The avatar made him feel flawed, but now he wondered if the avatar was defective.

So far, Falyn didn't seem as if she would reject him. She did kiss him back, and there were sparks. He was reluctant to project a future with her because one kiss didn't mean she would accept him as her mate.

The long walk back to her homestead should give them time to learn more about each other.

As he reached the creek, he jumped down from the bank to the water's edge. It was only several inches deep, but he managed to fill half a bucket. He jogged back to Falyn and the horse without spilling any.

Angus looked up from grazing as Max approached and held the bucket for him to drink. The horse drank most of it and then went back to grazing.

Carrying the bucket over to where Falyn sat on her open sleeping bag, he set it by the tree. "May I join you?"

"Sure." She patted the fabric next to her.

Max sat down beside her. "He drank about two liters. I will give him some time, then get more."

"If he is filling up on grass, he probably won't want more for a while."

"I can keep watch if you want to try to get some rest."

"I'd appreciate that. Now that you mention it, I feel pretty tired now that the adrenaline surge is over." Falyn lay down on her side, resting her head against the saddle. She took a deep breath and let it out, quickly falling   asleep.

Chapter Four

While Falyn slept, Max checked in with Captain Savage to let him know he'd found his mate. The captain suggested he could delay starting his job for a month. Max decided to take him up on it but still planned to scout a location for his new base of operations before that.

Next, he shared the news with the other members of his team. He did that not to brag but to encourage them that it was possible for them, too. It only took him a few minutes to communicate with the other five cyborgs over their network.

Then there was nothing much to do until daylight except to bring more water to the horse. While the horse could now walk that far, the bank was a four-foot drop from the creek bed. Max didn't want to risk the strain on its healing leg.

Rather than boredom, Max was happy to sit by Falyn and watch her sleep while he memorized her face and form. He kept looping through his CPU that she was the mate he had hoped for all his life.

The scientists who created them could have compiled a database of family lines for their genetic mates. Almost every aspect of human existence was in the data cloud on Earth. But the Enclave was too busy cranking out cyborgs to fight the war. Fellow cyborgs were disappointed and angry, believing they'd been betrayed. They learned it wasn't deliberate when the rangers returned to Earth. Buried deep in the database, they found a treatise detailing why it wasn't done.

Too many people were killed or displaced in the bombings. The power grids went down and took mass communications with them. The war they fought for *'her'* made it harder than they expected to find *'her.'*

Max smiled, silently rejoicing that he had found his mate and she was attracted to him. But he worried. Would she want him when she found out he was flawed? Or was he? The avatar, though AI-driven, wasn't a real human female. He shook his head.

Saving her horse already went a long way toward winning her favor. She clearly valued it as more than just a work animal. Watching her hold its head in her lap while stroking it tenderly and encouraging him with softly spoken words filled him with longing.

Lying with his head on her lap while she spoke soft words of endearment, stroking his close-cropped blond hair, was as close to the definition of heaven as he could get. Max didn't allow himself to think about breeding her. That would only make his pants seem uncomfortably tight again.

Falyn indicated she'd need time to adjust to the idea that he was her cyborg mate. Or maybe that he was a cyborg. She didn't seem to understand that even though he explained it.

Even while running through their relationship possibilities, he was hyperaware of their surroundings. If those men chasing her earlier were human traffickers, they wouldn't give up so easily.

Max heard the sound of horses trotting as he was halfway between the creek and where Falyn was just getting up. He ran full speed across the field, reaching them as two men from the day before tried to subdue her and tie her hands behind her back.

"Let her go!" Max roared.

Still, on their horses, the two men pointed ancient rifles at him, loading rounds in their firing chambers. "You stand down," said the apparent leader.

Max swung the bucket of water and hit the man on the right in the head with it so hard he fell off his horse. The cyborg pivoted, grabbed that man's rifle barrel, and yanked the rider to the ground. He hit one of the men holding Falyn in the head with the stock, then punched the other man in the face as he reached for his sidearm, a pistol.

Still conscious, the leader pulled out a pistol and shot Max in the back of the head. Max grunted, turned, kicked the gun from his hand, and then kicked him in the head as he tried to get up.

Touching the back of his head where the bullet hit him, he winced at the sting. The slug only went through the soft tissue and ricocheted. His scalp was bleeding, but his internal nanites rushed to close the wound.

Wiping his hand on his shirt, he turned and gripped Falyn's upper arms, examining her with sight and scanning her to make sure she was not injured.

"I'm okay," she murmured with a stunned expression.

"I had a feeling they hadn't given up. Stay right here. I'm going to put them in cuffs. Then I need to figure out what to do with them."

Falyn nodded.

Max went to his hidden sky cycle, pulled four zip ties from his cargo compartment, and cuffed the four downed men's hands behind their backs. Now he needed somewhere to hold them. His protector team wasn't due to arrive for another three weeks.

But Stalker's teams had already been there for a few weeks and had established a holding place for those who weren't amenable to the new order.

"Stalker, I need your help."

"Sure, Max. What can I do for you?"

"I have four thugs who just tried to kidnap my female."

"Processed. Your teams haven't arrived, and you don't have anywhere to hold them. Give me your coordinates, and I will send a hover transport for them."

"Thank you, I will wait for them to arrive and ask if Falyn can contain their horses."

"You're welcome. Also, Neely wants to meet your female when you are ready. She said she wants to compare notes, whatever that means."

"I will let you know after we have had some time to bond."

Acceptable. Stalker out.

"Max, is that your blood on your shirt? Are you hurt?" Falyn asked when he returned from securing the would-be kidnappers.

"It's nothing. That man shot me in the back of my head with his useless projectile pistol. It broke the skin before it bounced off my skull."

Max reached up and cupped his hand against her cheek. "That you are unhurt is more important than a minor puncture wound. They are lucky they didn't hurt you. I would have killed them all."

He was deadly serious, she realized. Seeing him dispatch four thugs, hardly breaking a sweat, was hot.

Falyn cupped her hand against Max's. She had heard of cyborgs before, but that was in the abstract. The reality was pretty damned impressive. Tall, fair-haired, and powerfully built. He was not just pretty. He was sexy with a capital S, or maybe it was those pheromones he told her about.

The blatant adoration in his intense gaze sent an unspoken invitation straight to her core. Her nipples tightened, and her inner walls clenched. She wanted him, and the slight lift at the corners of his mouth told her that he knew it.

Then he seemed to mentally shake himself, letting his hand drop from her cheek. "Do you have a fenced pasture where we could contain these four horses, at least temporarily?"

She nodded. "They can pasture with Angus as long as they aren't aggressive."

"Ain't none of these horses aggressive," said the man Max had hit with the bucket. "They's all good animals."

"Who are you, and why were you trying to kidnap this female?"

"I'm Maynard Carter. Driscoll, our boss said we had to bring in ten young and pretty females by the end of the week if we wanted supplies to feed our families."

"What's he doing with them?"

"He's got some alien slave broker auctioning them to off-worlders. We only have three more days to get four more."

"Give me the names of the other three," Max demanded.

"I don't think I should... probably shouldn't'a give mine."

"It doesn't matter; you're all going to jail for human trafficking, attempted kidnapping, assault with a deadly weapon for the one over there who shot me."

"But I can't go to jail. I got a wife and two kids. They won't have nobody to take care of them," Maynard protested. "She's pretty and young enough; Driscoll might just take her and my kids and sell them to the aliens. I gotta stop him! They ain't done nothing to deserve that."

"But you see no irony, taking a random female from wherever you find and sending her to be sold to aliens as a slave?"

"Uh…Ah… I don't think about it. They ain't nothin' to me."

"And that's the problem. Selling humans into slavery is a Federation offense. That will get you sent to the prison planet."

"Oh, man! Eldon is going to be pissed. He's got two mostly growed girls. When we don't come through, Driscoll will take them too.

"Not if we get there first. They will be safe if we get to them. The Enclave is taking back this Territory. The people living in the ruins will all get new homes as they are built, and Enclave teams will teach them how to homestead and become self-sufficient.

Chapter Five

Max finished questioning the four gang members well before Stalker's team arrived to pick them up. He left them sitting on the ground back-to-back with their hands cuffed behind them to join Falyn, where she had the four extra horses strung together.

"I almost feel bad for them and their families. Then, I remind myself they were planning to sell me to aliens," Falyn mused.

"Exactly. Unfortunately, we can only charge them with attempted kidnapping and assault. They probably won't go to the prison planet. They are cooperating, so they could be sentenced to labor for the Enclave helping to rebuild the towns and remain with their families," Max explained, speaking softly, so the captives didn't hear. "They are just lackies in Driscoll's operation. They told me where to find him, and there is a secret base where fake merchant ships land."

"What about their families?"

"Driscoll gave them till the end of the week to make their quota. I will have them evacuated before that. Stalker has an old military base where he's housing people waiting for new homes."

"That sounds good. Do you have to go with his people to secure these four?" Falyn knew she could handle the horses but wanted more time with Max. Something special was happening between them.

Her family had all passed on, and she had been alone on her homestead for eight years. Falyn didn't get many visitors because her place was far from town. She'd had a couple of good scares when some males showed up during that time. She was sure they planned to get a free meal and take turns raping her. She ran them off with her shotgun.

Fortunately, they had never been back.

"No. Stalker's team can handle it. As soon as they leave, I will help you walk the horses to your homestead," he assured her. "Stalker found his mate weeks ago. We have barely begun getting acquainted."

Falyn smiled at him. "I was hoping you would be able to come. Even with your help, it will take hours."

Max gave her a shy smile. "I was counting on that. I've waited a hundred years to find you. Now that I have, I want to know everything about you...."

He would have said more, but they were interrupted by the whine of the hover transport coming in to land in the meadow.

"Let me get these gangers loaded, and then we will go to your home."

Falyn watched him walk confidently toward the hovercraft. He moved with the grace of a mountain lion with broad shoulders, a narrow waist, a tight butt, and muscular arms and thighs.

She imagined how it would feel to be pressed against that muscular male chest with those strong arms wrapped around her.

This cyborg was different from other men she had known. He seemed almost innocent, as though he had no clue how to flirt or play courtship games. He knew she was his match as though it was a done deal.

Yet, there was tenderness tempering heat in his gaze, and she liked it. He didn't try to hide this from her. That must be what it meant to be genetic mates.

She didn't know much about genetics because her education hadn't included much about science that didn't pertain to homesteading. With the power grid and mass communications shut down decades before she was born, her family had only a collection of actual books to teach her to read and write.

The most important books were about homesteading, gardening, and animal care. Falyn's ancestors had lived mostly off the grid before the Mesaarkan attack on the cities. Now the isolated homestead belonged to her.

She liked the prospect of having a big handsome male to share her life... And the ongoing work of keeping up the homestead.

Did she dare to jump into this relationship wholeheartedly? She'd taken a leap of faith before and was wrong. She'd run that male off at gunpoint. There hadn't been a male in her life since.

Falyn saddled Angus while Max helped the Protectors get the four gangers secured in the transport. It only took a few minutes, and then they were gone.

"How do you want to do this?" Max asked.

"I put Angus's saddle on him, then I'm going to ride the lead horse and tether Angus at the back."

"We could hook Angus to my hovercycle, and I'll ride alongside you. I can go as fast or as slow as you need."

"That will be possible once we get to the old road. The trail through the woods is too narrow for that."

Max came to stand in front of her. "If that's what we have to do." Then he fell silent, just staring at her. It might have seemed creepy with anyone else, but Falyn found herself staring at his handsome face.

He stared at her lips longingly but didn't make a move. It seemed as though he wanted to kiss her. She wanted his kiss, but he seemed rooted to the spot.

Falyn waited only a couple seconds more, then she stepped forward, leaning into him and putting her arms around his neck. Raising up on her toes, she pulled his head down and brushed his mouth with her lips. She did it a few times, soft butterfly kisses. He took her into his arms, lifting her off her feet, and kissed her with a passion simmering just under the surface.

She opened readily when he slipped the tip of his tongue between her lips. Although she made the first move, Max quickly took control, deepening the kiss while urging her to wrap her legs around his hips.

Their first kiss was nice, but this was so sensual and arousing that her whole body clamored for more. His tongue swirled around hers in an erotic dance, alternately caressing and dominating.

Falyn clung to his shoulders, pressing her taut, aching nipples tighter against his hard chest. She vaguely wondered if this had been a wise move, but it felt right. Heat pooled at the juncture of her thighs and dampened her panties.

She wanted to keep going... get naked and have him fill her with his cock and pound into her until they were both fully sated. It seemed crazy even as she thought it. But it also felt right.

They were both panting when Max lifted his lips from hers.

"How did you know?" he murmured.

"Because I wanted it, too. Is that what it means to be genetic mates?"

"It's why we are attracted to each other," he admitted.

Falyn brought her hand up and caressed his cheek with the backs of her fingers. Kissing his lips lightly, she hugged him, then unwrapped her legs from around him and pressed herself away from him.

"We need to take care of these horses," she said with a wistful sigh.

They tied two horses to Max's sky cycle, and Falyn mounted the horse she had chosen and led the other horses tethered to the utility rope she carried. Max followed her on the narrow trail, at a safe distance behind. The sky cycle didn't make enough noise at that slow speed to bother the horses.

It was slow going up the narrow trail, but they made a little better time traveling on the crumbling old road. Following the same game trail that Falyn took to escape the gangers was a shortcut, they made it to her homestead in about three and a half hours.

Maynard was not lying about their horses being good animals. They were gentle and well-trained. When they reached her homestead, she and Max took them to the small barn to unsaddle them.

"We'll leave their bridles on while we lead them into the pasture and show them where the water is. Then we'll turn them loose."

Falyn only had three saddle stands, so they doubled up the extra saddles on two of them. Nor did she have halters for them, but she didn't anticipate having to catch them in a hurry. All she had for Angus was fashioned from a twisted synthetic rope.

Max checked Angus's leg one more time before Falyn turned him loose. "My scan barely showed where the break was. He should be fine."

"I'm so glad you could help him. It was breaking my heart to put him down." She released the horse, smiling at Max.

"I am happy to help."

"What's going to happen to these other horses?"

"I'll return them to their families if possible, but it may be a while. We will evacuate their families when the protectors arrive so this Driscoll can't traffic them."

"Then you're going after Driscoll?"

"Yes, soon. We need to find out who's over Driscoll. Stalker and I think it's the Mesaarkan, especially all the alien tech Stalker's team found in Los Angeles."

"You think an alien is here on Earth?"

"I do. Before Commander Dark came back, the Federation fleet was stretched pretty thin. It would have been easy for them to land here without anyone knowing. If Mesaarkans are here, they can't mingle without calling attention to themselves. They are reptilian with scales and tails."

Chapter Six

"You mean like lizards?" Falyn asked, wrinkling her nose.

Max nodded. "I think that is an apt description. Their faces are flatter and more human-like, but you would never mistake one for a human."

"What if they are here? What then?"

"Our treaty says we can only expel them from Earth. We can't ship them to the prison planet."

"Why would they want to come here after they've all but destroyed Earth?"

"Human trafficking is very lucrative. Apparently, some Mesaarkans have human fetishes."

"Fetishes?"

"They are obsessed with tormenting and copulating with human females."

"Oh," she responded, blushing. "My education is limited. Deviant behavior was not a subject I studied."

"I can help with your education... Not about deviant behavior...." He grinned. "I have com-tablets to give out to people in my territory. You can get on the AI net as well as communicate with anyone on the planet who has one.

Max stopped at his vehicle and opened the cargo compartment. The device he took out was about four inches square and unfolded into a few different configurations.

"That would be wonderful!" Falyn smiled up at him as he showed it to her. "I worry sometimes living up here alone with no neighbors. If I had an accident and needed help, I could be long dead before anyone found me."

"You won't need to worry any longer. You will have this." He handed it to her, "and me."

"Even if I don't become your mate?"

The hurt look that flashed in his eyes made Falyn regret taunting him, especially after he had been so nice fixing Angus's leg after she shot him.

And more so when he said, "even then."

Falyn stopped and turned to him, resting a hand on his upper arm. "I'm not saying I won't…." She paused, shaking her head. "I was teasing. I'm sorry. It wasn't funny." As she stroked his arm, his expression softened. "I like you and think you might be a good mate. I just want to get better acquainted before we take the next step."

"For me, it's you or no one." Max framed her face in his hands and then smoothed her hair, nodding. "I understand it's different for you. I was programmed to become your mate and make a family with you. But you didn't know anything about me until yesterday." He rested his hands on her shoulders and held her gaze.

Falyn liked the warmth in his blue eyes. "Do cyborgs eat?"

"Yes, we do. We can go long periods without nourishment, but we like to eat regularly.

"Good, I will make us some breakfast. I just need to stop at the henhouse and collect a few eggs. I'll probably have to fire up the cook stove. The coals have probably burnt out as I've been gone so long."

"That sounds nice." The corners of his lips lifted briefly, and his eyes sparked with appreciation. It didn't hurt that he was one of the most gorgeous men she had ever seen. Everything about him was alluring, and he smelled so good.

"I might have some bread from the other day," she murmured as they stopped by the hen house. "Hold this." Falyn handed him the tablet, opening the outer door to the hens' nests. Since she didn't have her egg basket, she pulled up her tunic for a pouch, collecting the eggs into it.

One month earlier

"Fuck!" Colton Price growled, slapping the console of the stolen flyer. There was no way he could get the Mesaarkan flyer back. He hadn't counted on Neely coming to Stalker's defense when he tried to steal back the last of the three Mesaarkan flyers.

Then he had to laugh. She'd burst out the front door stark naked and stunned him with her blaster when he was about to kill her mate. He didn't understand why she hadn't killed him.

Maybe because they had once been allies of sorts. He'd done her a favor shooting down her flyer, though even he didn't know it at the time. It landed her right in the lap of her genetic cyborg mate.

Colton had gone there to steal the Mesaarkan flyer, not kill anyone. He had only been armed just in case... Stalker surprised him, and he was a better fighter and stronger. But Stalker tripped, ironically, over the piece of machinery he'd thrown at Colton.

One stab of the Mesaarkan radial knife disabled Stalker. Colton regained consciousness before Neely returned with the nanites to treat her mate. He let his emotions steer him to the wrong choice.

He was going to kill Stalker to punish Neely for getting in his way, and he wasted time searching for the knife she had taken inside. Colton could have stolen the flyer in the time he wasted on intent to kill Stalker.

When Neely came back, her blaster was set to kill. The look in her eyes told him she would kill him as she said it. Stalker's gasp gave him the seconds he needed to get away.

Devlin White's luxury flyer would get him where he needed to go. Maybe Thrix could have it retrofitted with weapons.

With the Enclave cyborgs moving in, Colton didn't know how long they could operate in the San Francisco area. The cyborgs they were sending would start rooting out the gangers and bosses. Van'Rel Thrix would have to move or be discovered and deported.

As a Mesaarkan, Thrix could not be sent to prison even for human trafficking. According to the treaty, they could only expel and banish him from Earth. The Federation agreed to that stipulation because employees from an Earth conglomerate started the war. They massacred Mesaarkan settlers on a planet they wanted for mining rights. They would send Colton to the prison planet if they caught him, or he could end up dead.

He was positive Devlin White had sent his wife Tessa to Thrix with the gutter rats he pulled from the ruins. Those people lived like animals, the sludge of humanity. At least, that's what Colton told himself to justify his betrayal.

He became a Federation Agent, hoping to find Tessa or avenge her if she was dead. White was never going to tell him what he'd done. Killing the bastard felt so good that he wished he could do it again and watch the light fade from his eyes as he twisted the knife.

For all he knew, Thrix could have Tessa stashed somewhere with his personal stock. He'd asked the Mesaarkan, but that lizard claimed he couldn't tell them apart. Colton didn't believe that.

He had wasted so much time looking for her in the East when White had probably sent Tessa out West with one of his shipments to the Mesaarkan connection.

Colton was done with that game. The Federation didn't need him to find the traffickers. Their thousands of manufactured cyborgs could do it. Now that he'd gone rogue, they would come for him, too.

Van'Rel Thrix went through the reports on his virtual AI screen on the desk in front of him. Things weren't going so well since they moved cyborgs into his region. He'd had free reign here for about ten years. Now the cyborgs were dismantling his whole operation in the Los Angeles region. The humans collected for auction were all liberated. Gods curse them!

He hated humans. They were vile creatures, but they served him in this business. They were all males. He only found pleasure in using the females for his recreational activities.

He always enjoyed that first encounter when a new female saw him without his human disguise. He was, in fact, handsome by Mesaarkan standards. Mesaarkans were bi-pedal humanoids in varied shades from light tan to black and covered in scales.

While humans called them lizards, their heads and facial features were somewhat human-like. Their eyes were more prominent in their skulls, and their brow line was ridged. Unlike actual lizards, they had lips and nostrils, but their noses were much flatter.

Van'Rel was tall, green, and muscular with a long prehensile tail and a carnal appetite for human females. He had a room in his dwelling; he called his recreation room— the alien equivalent of a BDSM dungeon.

He used it to train the females for service to their Mesaarkan masters before shipping them out. First, he made them scream in pain, then he made them scream in pleasure. He so enjoyed his job. But there was one female who he was claiming for himself.

He was finishing the reports when his assistant knocked softly on his door.

"Enter." Van'Rel shut down his computer interface.

"Colton Price is here to see you."

"Did he say why?"

"He's looking for his female. He thinks Devlin White sent her here with one of his shipments," his assistant said.

"Send him in. I'll talk to him. In the meantime, would you set Connie up in the rec room? Then report back to me."

"As you wish, sir." The Mesaarkan servant left the room, and momentarily Colton strode into the office.

"Good day, Thrix. I need to see your harem. White might have shipped my mate to you in one of the groups he sent before I got back on Earth. I've been to every harem and brothel run by the eastern Overlords, and none of them had her."

"Do you even know that she is alive and didn't just run away?

"I don't know that she is dead, but I do know she wouldn't just run away. If White was short on a shipment, he could have put her into it to fill his quota."

"I asked White, but he gave me some crap that she probably left because he hadn't seen her in a while. I know she wouldn't have left of her own accord. She was excited that I was coming home."

Thrix almost felt sorry for him, as he seemed truly distraught over the loss of his mate. "I will have Za'Ras escort you through the harem and take you to the holding barracks. If your mate is among them, we will work it out."

"Thank you, Van'Rel." Colton dipped his head as a sign of respect, and Za'Ras returned momentarily.

As Colton left with Za'Ras, his mouth compressed into a thin line, and he shook his head. Could Connie be the female the human sought? …The one female he wouldn't give up?

He hoped not for Colton's sake. The cyborg convert was one of the few humans he almost liked. Van'Rel would find killing him at least distasteful, but he would if it meant keeping Connie.

She screamed and cried while he punished her, yet she almost relished the pain, and she rarely begged for it to stop like the other females. She could take it so much longer than the others before he pleasured her.

His cock hardened inside his slit. Van'Rel needed release soon. What was it about this female that the thought of fucking her did this to him? He wasn't the only Mesaarkan who liked to screw human females. That's why procuring them and selling them had made him wealthy.

Colton didn't need to know Van'Rel held one female back when he let the cyborg see his harem. He wasn't taking the chance that Colton would claim her as his female.

Chapter Seven

"Mm," said Max, spearing another bite of omelet with his fork. "I don't often get to eat freshly made food. This is wonderful."

Falyn smiled, enjoying his praise. "It's just eggs, vegetables, and some goat cheese."

"I'm just sorry, this is all the bread left. I used the last of my flour to make it; it will be another month until I can harvest the wheat patch. But I have some garbanzos to grind and make bread."

"You're talking to a male who lives on meal bars and nutrient drinks. During the war, we often ate insects for fresh meat. You don't need to deplete your food supply for me."

Max knew they were skirting the subject of their mating, but he knew not to push her. He could smell her arousal, and he surmised she knew it because of her pinkening cheeks.

Max was unsure whether he should speak openly about it or keep talking around it until Falyn seemed more at ease. His cock was so hard that he wanted to ask her to breed, but he couldn't get the words out. Her avatar said he never gave her a choice; he just seduced her. Other cyborgs didn't have such incidents with their avatar mates. His had deliberately hurt him with her disdainful insults and frequent berating. Falyn seemed nothing like her avatar except in her appearance. Pulling himself back from the past, he continued the conversation.

"From what I can see, your homestead is well maintained and self-sufficient. You have solar panels and a windmill with an electric cooler and a cooker, yet you cook on an ancient wood stove."

"Because I am trying to conserve the batteries for the fridge. They are very old, and some no longer hold a charge. This used to be my great, great grandfather's off-the-grid vacation home. The town where he lived was not bombed, but the bombings cut off utilities and communications. So, he packed up his family and moved them here."

"Did he prepare all this before the bombings?" asked Max.

"He did. My family called him a prepper. He never trusted the Earth Alliance because they were always squabbling. He believed one country or another would start a war." Falyn paused, meeting his gaze. "We never knew the attack came from off-world... Although we wondered, I never knew until you told me."

"How do you take care of all this yourself?" he asked. It was a small property by farm standards, about a dozen acres.

"I have some machines that still work. Of course, they cannibalized the fuel cells from the hovercraft to keep them running. A cultivator bot tills and weeds, and I have a harvester bot.

"Heck, living alone here for all this time, there is nothing else to do, and certainly not if I want to survive."

Noting he had finished eating, Falyn got up from her chair at the kitchen table, gathering the plates and tableware, leaving only the empty mugs. She carried them to the sink and quickly washed and rinsed them, placing them in the drainer. On her way back, she took the tea kettle from the stove, came to the table, and poured hot herbal tea into their mugs.

"This is mixed herbal tea. I pick it, dry it, and blend it myself." Falyn reached for a small jar of amber syrup. "It will taste better if you stir in a spoon of honey. It's one of the things I trade for in town with some beekeepers."

"What do you trade?" Max took the honey jar as she passed it to him, took a spoonful, and stirred it into his beverage.

"Anything I can think of: vegetables in season, eggs if I have extras, cheese, goatmilk soap, herbs. I learned how to make all that from my mom and dad. They were always thankful that great-great-grandfather stocked this place with books that told us how to do all of this."

"Those are excellent skills to have. Everything you have here is what the Enclave wants to teach the urban dwellers," he said. "Perhaps you could help with that after they clear away the wreckage in the cities and rebuild."

"Are there enough people to rebuild cities?"

Max shook his head. "They will be settlements of homesteaders like yourself."

They chatted on the subject while they drank their tea until things fell into an awkward silence. They sat staring at each other, almost mesmerized by the sexual tension reverberating between them.

Falyn knew he wanted her by his longing gaze, yet he didn't say anything. What was he waiting for? Her one and only sexual encounter was less than stellar, over almost as soon as it started. It had been his first time too. His family had been their nearest neighbor, about two miles away.

They had been lonely teenagers. Jesse thought he loved her. He was a good kisser, though, and good with his hands, so it seemed logical to go to the next step. Her father found out, and she didn't see Jesse after that.

What she felt with Max, who was also good at kissing, was much more intense. It was becoming hard to sit still. He looked at least as tightly wound as she felt. Why wouldn't he just say what he wanted? Did he expect her to just know? The unspoken question was on his face, but he couldn't or wouldn't say the words.

This was what the avatar must have been scolding him for. They were genetic mates; sex was the logical progression of their relationship. She knew it wasn't love that was driving the attraction between them. It was biologically driven by those pheromones, whatever they were.

Falyn finally pushed her chair out and stood. Max pushed his chair back but looked to her for instruction. With a playful smirk, Falyn decided what to do.

She walked to his side of the table, slid between Max and the table, and sat down on his lap, facing him. She stifled a moan as she felt his hard cock against her pussy through their clothes.

Falyn slid her hand over his shoulders and around his neck, kissing his mouth lightly. "I want you, and you want me," she whispered. "Are we going to do anything about it?"

"You wish to breed?" he asked, his breath coming a little faster.

"Don't you?" she countered. It flared in his eyes before he got the words out.

"Yes, I do.

"Then let's get naked and do it." She laughed and kissed him in earnest.

Max might be shy with words, but he wasn't shy about taking her mouth with his tongue. They kissed long and deeply, Falyn rocking over his erection and pressing her aching breasts tightly against his hard chest. She felt that kiss all the way to her toes, and her core clenched.

When they parted lips, Falyn said, "My bedroom is down that little hall across the living room. That is where I wish to breed." *Fuck me long and hard.*

She started to get up. "No, let me," Max murmured. He stood, gripping her buttocks. "Put your legs around me, and I will take you there." She liked that idea even better and did as he asked.

Falyn smiled and laid her head on his shoulder, hugging him. "It's the open doorway at the end."

"I see it."

And so did she. Her big strong cyborg mate was painfully shy, at least with her.

Max didn't let her down immediately, so Falyn raised her head from his shoulder to look into his eyes.

"You are so beautiful!" he assured her, pressing his lips to hers. His kiss was at first sweet and tender, as if he was infusing it with the seeds of love germinating inside him.

Falyn caressed his head and face, sighing as his kiss grew more passionate, their tongues dueling sensually. Max held her tightly, running his hands over her back and shoulders throughout the long, slow kiss. He felt wonderful in her arms and so right.

When he set her on her feet beside the bed, she paused, looking up at him to see if he intended to assist her in undressing. He seemed content to let her take the lead, so she pulled her tunic top off over her head and dropped it on the floor.

"Now, your turn," she said. "Take off your shirt."

He pulled it from his black cargo pants' waistband and slid it off his head. His chest was a work of art with chiseled abs, bulging pecs, and biceps. There was just a faint indentation in the middle of his chest where she had shot him.

Feeling a pang of guilt, she stepped close and kissed that fading scar. That emboldened Max to frame her face in his hands and tilt her head to meet his gaze. "I'm okay. You didn't know I wasn't there to hurt you. I never want to hurt you."

"And I know that now."

"I want you so much," Max whispered and kissed her, caressing her lips with his.

"Then let's do this." Falyn took a small step back when the kiss ended to resume undressing.

Falyn's bra was a length of fabric wound around her chest to support her breasts, tied in a bow in the front. Her trousers were made from a coarsely woven fabric with a drawstring at the waist. Instead of panties, she had a strip of cloth tied at the waist on each side. Her shoes were handmade leather moccasins with leather laces to hold them on, but Falyn toed them off before she dropped her pants.

Max no longer seemed shy or reluctant to strip off his pants and boots.

She stared at him for seconds, and slowly smiled. Well-muscled and well hung, she hadn't doubted it but seeing him in all his naked glory was breathtaking.

"Oh, Max! You are magnificent!" Falyn stepped closer and hugged him, pressing her naked body to his.

Chapter Eight

Max closed his eyes and wrapped his arms around Falyn, hugging her back, simply basking in the joy of holding his mate. She was accepting him. She wanted him!

They held each other for a few moments, then Falyn leaned back, looking up at him as she ran her hands up over his chest, clasped them at the back of his neck, and tilted her face up with parted lips, silently asking for his kiss.

Max wasted no time obliging. He lifted her up, so they were chest to chest with his length pressed between them. Unable to touch the floor, she wrapped her legs around him. The pressure of her mons against his hard cock felt good as he savored kissing her.

His only 'experience' with sex was in his virtual life with his mate's avatar. He learned many ways to satisfy his flesh and blood mate from her. When the kiss ended, he slowly let her slide down his body until she stood on the floor.

Falyn stroked his chest and gave him an appreciative smile before she turned back the bed covers and moved onto the bed. Besides the one sexual encounter, Falyn had learned about sex and sexual pleasure from an ancient book on human sexuality in her grandfather's collection how to satisfy a lover.

Until now, she had only experienced pleasure by her own hand. None of the offers from the townsmen struck her fancy. Some of them were downright scary. She was a little nervous, but something about Max made her feel that she could trust him.

Falyn lay on her back at the bed's center, Max lay over her, his leg between her thighs against her pussy. Holding his weight above her on his forearms, he studied her face with wonder.

She was so touched by his apparent devotion that she reached up and caressed his face. Falyn could relate because she felt much the same. This big, handsome man drops out of the sky at one of her life's darkest moments and saves her and her horse. Those reasons might make her want to be amenable to breeding with him. Almost from the moment they met, this magnetism drew them to this moment.

"My beautiful, Falyn. I only want to give you pleasure. You are the one I've waited for all my life."

"I want to please you too. Ever since I got close to you, I wanted this… I want *you*."

He smiled and planted little kisses over her face, pausing at her mouth for a deeply arousing kiss as their tongues caressed and explored.

When it finished, Falyn's nipples and clit throbbed for attention. But Max was not in a hurry to get to the main event. He seemed bent on worshiping her entire body with his lips and tongue, adding a little nip here and there. She read a few old romances that described explicit sex, but she never imagined how her whole body would quiver with need.

Max was doing this, making her gasp, mew, and moan with delight. She purred his name in breathy sighs, caressing his head and upper body wherever she could reach.

He took his time enjoying and pleasuring her breasts, nipping and sucking her nipples until she positively writhed, voicing her pleasure without words. She adored how intent he was on pleasing and arousing her as he left her nipples throbbing.

Planting little kisses and dropping licks over her ribs and abdomen, he raised on all fours to move between her legs and resumed worshiping her body. As he dragged his mouth down her belly, she caught her breath as she suspected his intent.

Gazing at her pussy, he parted the hair to get a better look, breathing in her musk. Pressing his fingertip on her sensitive clit, caused her pussy to clench as she let out a moan.

Pushing up her legs so he could grip her thighs, he lowered his face and drew his tongue up her channel and over her clit. Settling his mouth over it, he teased the sensitive bud with his tongue while he inserted a finger and then another into her opening."

"Omigod, Omigod..." was the most coherent noise Falyn made before screaming in ecstasy as Max took her sailing over the edge of pure bliss. Just when it seemed to end, he flicked the tip of his tongue over her clit, and her body seized in orgasm again. She finally pushed him back when she became too sensitive to take any more.

Max paused to wipe his face, then moved back up to lay over her, staring down into her eyes. Falyn brought her hands up to caress his face. What she saw in his eyes was tender; it made her want to give him everything. She whispered his name and pulled him down to kiss her, tasting herself on his lips and not minding at all.

After a brief, tender kiss, he said, "I need you now...."

"Yes, I'm ready," she whispered, knowing this would make her his. He'd explained all that on the journey back to the homestead. Maybe it was reckless to accept this cyborg male as her mate. Yet, after eight years of fending for herself alone, she couldn't return to that. Not only was she attracted to him, she liked him and could see herself falling in love with him.

Max was handsome, strong, and kind enough to repair Angus's broken leg. His kisses made her whole body clamor for him to take her. By committing to be his, he would be hers.

He balanced on one forearm, poised his cock at her entrance, and slid easily into her slick tunnel to the hilt. Even so, he was big, and it was a tight fit, but it felt so good, and she moaned her pleasure.

Falyn liked the weight of his big body pressing down on her as he kissed her. She was completely in the moment, giving and receiving pleasure. Nothing and no one else existed, but the man in her arms joined to her. She caressed him, running her hands up and down his back, telling him without words that he pleased her.

His mouth barely left here as he raised and lowered his hips so that nearly every stroke rubbed her clit. Tilting her pelvis up to meet him, she was enthralled by the male fucking her.

Once when their lips parted, she looked up into his dark eyes as he claimed her with every thrust of his cock.

Falyn murmured his name, filled with overwhelming affection. She raised her hand to caress his face, hyperaware of every nuance in his expression. He kissed her again, and her hands moved to his lower back, pressing him to her on the downward plunge.

That was just the introduction. As she wished he would fuck her harder and faster, he did just that, pounding into her so fast she could no longer match his thrusting.

But it was exhilarating, taking her through two more orgasms before he found release. Falyn reached the third release as Max roared, shooting his hot seed inside her. She inadvertently dug her nails in his back as powerful contractions shuddered through her.

Max seemed not to notice in the throes of his own orgasm. As they both came down from their mutual release, he pulsed his cock inside her, sending little aftershocks rippling through her body.

Holding her gaze, he tenderly caressed her face. He seemed deeply moved by what they had just shared.

Falyn knew she had made the right choice. She never wanted to share this kind of joining with anyone but Max.

"You are mine, and I am yours," Max said, the words he'd yearned to utter all his life.

"You are mine, and I am yours," she murmured. "From now on…."

"From now on," Max repeated. He pulled out of her and turned them on their sides, cuddling her close.

After a night short on sleep and the best sex she ever dreamed of, Falyn drifted to sleep in his arms.

Max didn't mind. She was his. All the years of fighting, going from planet to planet, every being he ever killed, was all for *her.* Not that defective avatar from his virtual life; he did it for Falyn. Now, she had a name, and he called her *mine.*

"You are mine," he said, pressing a kiss to her forehead. She was beautiful, and she accepted him. For the first time in his life, he felt truly happy.

Used to going up to a week at a time without sleep, Max wasn't that tired, but he closed his eyes and replayed his claiming of Falyn from his memory bank. He didn't know how their lives would fit together yet, but they would figure it out.

Had he found Falyn before he agreed to take North California, he would have passed on the promotion. Max couldn't see how she would work with him like Stalker's mate Neely. She'd spent her life homesteading. He wouldn't put her in danger like that.

Max doubted Falyn would want to, anyway. She wasn't that good with a gun. Homesteading was a lot of work. It wasn't like she'd have nothing to do while he was on the job. After what happened to Captain Savage's wife, Max would set up security on Falyn's homestead.

Nothing was more important to him than Falyn.

Chapter Nine

Falyn awoke about two hours later, and they made love again with less foreplay and more fucking. Afterward, they showered together, washing each other, leading to another round of sex with Falyn pressed against the shower wall. Once they'd gotten past their first time, they couldn't seem to get enough of each other.

By the time they finished showering and dressing, Falyn thought Max was getting over his initial shyness. However, she wondered how long it would have taken them had she not made her desire known. Could the glitch in his avatar have been a mistake, or had some sadistic programmer done it on purpose? But she didn't ask.

When they got dressed, the sourdough garbanzo bread she started after lunch was ready to bake. Stoking the fire in the wood cookstove, she put the bread in the oven to bake. Then she asked Max to go with her for evening chores so she could show him around. They started in her small barn to milk the goats.

Solar panels on the roof charged the batteries that ran the lights and her portable electric milker. There were three pygmy nannies and one buck, no bigger than a medium size dog.

"What was your childhood like?" Falyn asked as she lifted the little nanny onto a roughhewn milking table. Washing the nanny's udder and teats first with a wet cloth and then a spray, she hooked suction cups to its teats. The table was enclosed on three sides so the goat wouldn't step off. Falyn stood on the open side to keep the animal in place and monitor the milker.

"We experienced childhood in virtual reality through our internal computers," he explained. "It seemed real at the time. My parents were both in the military. My father was a strategist, and my mother was a medic. Since we were bred to fight in the war, I went to virtual military school."

"So, you had a family?"

"Not really. They were mainly background. At five years old, I went to virtual military school with the other cyborgs in my batch. They were the closest to a family I had. We were pulled from our gestation tanks full grown after five years."

"That's incredible! I grew up right here." Falyn hooked up one of the little nannies. "I was an only child because my brother was stillborn. The cord was wrapped around his neck, and he died before leaving the birth canal. Dad and I were the only ones here to help her. All we had were a book on midwifery and birthing from before the war."

"You remember that?"

"Yes. I was eight at the time. Speaking of birthing, I don't have access to contraceptives. I should not be ovulating for another week, but after that, I could likely become pregnant if we keep mating. I do want children, just not yet."

"We need time to grow our relationship before we bring children into it," Max filled in for her. "I will take care of it. I can program my nanites to suppress my sperm until we are ready."

"You can do that?" Falyn beamed at him. He nodded, looking all shy again.

"Can you also erase that avatar bitch who was such a messed-up version of me? I know we just met, but you don't have to hide from me. We have great sex, and I like you. That's as good a start to a relationship as any."

Before Falyn returned to her task, she caught Max's pleased expression. The only positive thing about the flawed avatar was that she could just be herself, and Max would still want her.

"Deleted."

Falyn knew he meant the avatar and gave him a warm smile. From the open admiration in his gaze, that seemed like a done deal.

"I'm surprised you have solar panels, electricity, and a milking machine for goats."

"That's because great-great-grandfather was a serious prepper. There was a lot of unrest in the world during his lifetime. He thought it was only a matter of time before something happened to take down civilization and leave us to fend for ourselves. He set up this homestead so we could fend for ourselves and thrive."

"You are here alone, though," Max observed.

"Yes," she said with a sigh. My parents died about four years apart… Dad first, then Mom. They got sick from things that would have been cured by state-of-the-art medicine in great grandpa's time. But they didn't have that. All we had was a few antibiotics and natural remedies. That's all I have, now."

"Not anymore," Max assured her. "You will have the same nanites that heal me to heal you. If you need more than that, I will get it."

Falyn stopped the milker when she saw it was no longer pulling any milk from the little goat. Unhooking it, she set the goat back on the barn floor. As she straightened to locate the next goat, Max slid his arms around her, pulling her against him. Falyn didn't discourage him, pleased to see that he was becoming confident to do so.

She put her arms around his neck and looked up at him expectantly. He didn't disappoint, bending to press his lips to hers in a light, affectionate kiss. Falyn smiled at him as he held her gaze afterward, realizing how much she enjoyed this gorgeous male.

Alas, she still had two more goats to milk, so she pulled back reluctantly to finish the job. She glanced at him intermittently, and he seemed content to watch her finish the chore.

Three little goats didn't produce much milk but more than enough for one person. When she finished the milking, she poured the milk from the stainless-steel canister through a filter in the milk room processor that would pasteurize and cool it. She would retrieve it later.

Next, she fed the chickens and collected the eggs. She would wait until dusk to feed the horses a measure of grain to give them the incentive to return to the barn. Keeping them in the barn at night would protect them from mountain lions and wolves.

Falyn stopped on the way back to the house to pick some fresh vegetables from the garden for dinner. She carried the eggs and some of the vegetables back to the house, and Max took the rest.

"The vegetables were an afterthought," she said as they walked. "I should have brought a basket."

"Next time," said Max. "This place is amazing... And you take care of it all by yourself?"

"I have an antique solar-powered garden combine that saves me a lot of work. It's fully automated once I set it."

"How did you get such a device? After the bombings, everything shut down."

"Great grandfather stocked a fleet of them before the war. He bought a new one every couple of years, but he never used the new ones until the old one didn't work anymore. Mine is the last one."

"What you have here is exactly what the Enclave has envisioned for the rebuilding. Homesteads like this are everywhere back east."

"From when I was old enough to walk practically, my entire education was homesteading. Reading and arithmetic were coincidentally useful for reading all our books on preserving, soap making, and caring for livestock."

"'I did notice the entire wall beside and above the fireplace in the living room was all bookshelves filled with books," said Max.

"Those plus working alongside my parents were my education. I haven't read them all, but I'm still working on it."

"That is quite a collection. You can access the latest information on the tablet I will give you."

They entered the house through the kitchen door. Falyn set the egg basket and the vegetables on the counter beside the sink. Max put the rest beside hers.

"I am going to my hybrid cycle to get that tablet for you. I want us to be able to contact each other while I'm on the job."

Falyn nodded. "I will wash these and start a stir fry."

She let out a sigh as he left. She wasn't looking forward to his leaving, wondering how long before she would see him again. Falyn knew she couldn't go with him to the ruined cities. They were far more dangerous than going to town, which hadn't worked so well this time.

She didn't know how to fight and wasn't that good with a gun. After shooting Max by accident, she didn't trust herself with one. It didn't matter. There was far too much work at the homestead for her to be away for more than a day.

With another sigh, she pumped water into a basin in the sink and started cleaning the vegetables.

Chapter Ten

"I have to leave tomorrow," Max said as they ate. "I should return by evening the day after. I will call you if it is longer."

"Okay. That doesn't sound too bad."

"Had I not committed to this job, I wouldn't leave. I have one hundred protectors arriving the day after tomorrow, and I still need to pick a place for our base."

"It sounds like you are going to be busy. I've never been to the cities, but I haven't heard good things about it from those who have," she told him.

"Some rangers and protectors take their mates with them on the job, but two females were badly injured. I won't put you in danger like that," Max assured her.

"Your need to protect me could put you at risk, and my work is here. I depend on this homestead to survive. But if there is any way I can help you, I will."

"Taking care of the gangers' horses is already helping." He took a bite of food, his eyes glinting with appreciation. "Once I get my protectors settled in and working the city, I hope to have more time to help you. I guess the first question is do you want to live here together, or would you like to have something new built?"

"Well, this is a four-bedroom house. I'll be happy to share it with you."

"As you wish, my mate." This time he smiled as if he was just happy to be with her sharing a simple meal.

Falyn could feel herself blushing as his gaze darkened with passion. Her body responded to that look and the memory of their earlier lovemaking. Her nipples tightened, and her core throbbed and clenched against emptiness.

She looked down at her plate as she speared some meat and vegetables onto her fork and brought them to her mouth. She would need the nourishment to keep up with her male's energetic mating. Oh, but she did love it!

After dinner, Falyn washed the dishes with homemade soap and left them to air dry on a wooden rack. The sun was just setting, so they went to the barn to get the horses inside.

She only had to call Angus, and he came trotting up to the barn, but she wasn't sure how to get the other horses to come.

Angus knew to come because she always gave him a small measure of grain or some carrots from the root cellar. When the other horses seemed content to stay at the far end of the pasture, Falyn said, "it looks like I might have to saddle up Angus and herd them in."

Max looked at the horses casually grazing at the far end of the pasture for seconds while accessing the AI net from his internal processors for a solution. "I can run out and herd them in."

"Okay." Falyn looked a bit skeptical but nodded. "I'll keep the barn door opened." Holding her horse by his halter, she watched Max jog across the field.

He jogged past where the other horses grazed and shooed them toward the barn. When one tried to turn back, Max raced to block it. As Falyn watched him, she realized he could run as fast as they did.

With the other horses headed in, she led Angus to his stall. As she gave her horse his treats, the other four horses trotted onto the walkway between the six stalls. Max closed the lower half of the barn door behind them.

Closing Angus in his stall, Falyn said, "They can go into any of these stalls." She opened the stall next to Angus and reached for the closest horse. Speaking to the chestnut gelding. She coaxed him into the pen with a hand under his head.

Watching Falyn, Max then followed suit. Maynard, the would-be kidnapper, was right. They were all nice horses and responded to a soothing tone and a gentle touch. Once inside the stalls, Max handed out carrots to them while Falyn measured out small scoops of grain.

"With this many horses, the grain won't last long," said Falyn.

"I will contact the Enclave and see where we can source more for you. Since this is related to the case, you won't have to pay for it. Their stay here should be temporary until I can find the families."

"What if you don't find them, or they don't want them? They're too well-mannered to just turn loose."

"We'll find someone else who can use them, who will care for them properly. It will be a while before more modern forms of transportation are widely available."

"That sounds good. I love my horse and horses, but I don't need four more."

"I've come to admire horses from my time in Montana. There are still places where they roam free."

"There are a few in the valley, I've heard, but they are most likely descended from tame horses left to fend for themselves."

"I have been thinking about learning to ride one, but I need a big strong one who can carry my weight."

"Probably a draft horse could carry you. But you don't look like you would be too heavy for any of these."

"I am over one-hundred pounds heavier than a natural male because of my enhancements. I'll have to ask Captain Savage where he found his horse," Max said. "Is there anything else we need to do for them?

"We just need to fill their water buckets. There is a hand pump at the watering trough outside."

It took another ten minutes to fill all the water buckets and distribute them. Next, Falyn put the little goats into the shed attached to the side of the barn. They would be easy prey for a coyote, and she couldn't afford to lose them.

With evening chores finished, Falyn turned to head back to the house, and Max caught her in his arms and pulled her against his hard body. It was as if he'd read her mind as she melted against him. More likely, he scented her arousal that she had been fighting since before dinner.

She knew she was quickly becoming infatuated with the big muscular cyborg, liking that he made her feel cared for when she was in his arms. Being with him made her happy.

Falyn had been alone so long; she hadn't realized she was lonely until Max buzzed into her life on his sky cycle. Until then, it was quickly becoming the worst day of her life as she contemplated putting down her beloved horse.

It was still surreal that this man had dropped into her life two days ago and she had essentially consented to be his wife. As she wound her arms around his neck, she smiled up at him, parting her lips in anticipation of his kiss.

The tender passion in his eyes as he lowered his head to claim hers in an ardent kiss made her want to give him everything. She thought she could kiss him for hours as their tongues tangoed sensually.

During their kiss, he lifted her to wrap her legs around his waist, carrying her back to the house. Then they were in her bedroom, pulling off their clothing, eager to come together. Max picked Falyn up when they were naked again, claiming another arousing kiss.

Falyn basked in the pleasure of his kiss while pressing her sensitive breasts against his muscular chest. Her clit throbbed, and her nipples ached for attention. Max seemed reluctant to part his lips from hers, so Falyn pressed little butterfly kisses on his lips and face until he leaned her back in his arms to latch on to her nipples with his mouth.

Max sucked on them alternately, driving her wild with desire until she came spontaneously against his belly. She didn't have to tell him she was ready for him to fuck her. She sighed relief as he got onto the bed with her still wrapped around him. He laid her down beneath him, kissing her, and she parted her legs so he could slide his cock into her, moaning as he did.

Falyn held him tenderly, caressing his head and back through the kiss. How could she feel this much ardor in such a short time? Or was it just so much better than being alone?

Seconds later, she no longer cared to question it. Max started pumping in and out of her, hard and deep, emphasizing his claim of her with each thrust. She gave a little huff, with each one tilting her pelvis upward to meet him. He was exquisitely hitting all the right places and stroking her inner walls, steadily driving her to another mind-blowing orgasm.

Soon he was pounding into her, and she adored the climb to ecstasy as he took her to climax twice before he poured his nanite-laden essence into her.

Afterward, she clung to him with his weight pressing down on her, still joined. Tomorrow he was leaving. She didn't want him to go. She couldn't deny the niggling fear that he wouldn't come back even through no fault of his own.

Chapter Eleven

By the time Falyn woke in the morning, Max had let the horses out to pasture, milked the goats, and collected the eggs from the chickens. She awoke to the smell of eggs cooking and emerged sleepily from the bedroom to find Max in the kitchen cooking them.

"Well, look at you," she said with a smile. "Not only great in bed, and you can cook, too. Definitely, a keeper."

"As late as I kept you up, I figured I could take care of things for you?" Max put down the wooden spatula and set the cast iron frying pan off the stove onto a wood cutting board.

Turning, he took her into his arms, kissed her with just a quick slip of his tongue, and hugged her. "I have never known such joy as I do, making love to you. I'm having trouble finding the will to leave you and do my job, but I must."

"Yes, I know the feeling. Being with you makes me realize how long it's been since I felt truly happy. I will miss you."

"As I will you… I suggest you keep your com-tablet handy. I don't think I will want to wait to call you until I know if I will be back tomorrow evening or not." Max held her a little longer, looking down at her as though memorizing her face. He let her go reluctantly. "We should eat while the eggs are still warm."

Falyn was about to set the kitchen table for them, but Max had done that, too. So, she sat at her place and watched him serve a large portion to each of their plates. There was already a pot of herbal tea and two mugs on the table as well.

"Thank you for doing all this. It's very sweet of you." She gave him an appreciative smile. It would be so hard to watch him go.

"I would do anything for you, my mate," he assured her.

She was sorely tempted to ask him to forget about his job and just stay there with her. But she couldn't. Max had a hundred protectors arriving tomorrow, and they would be looking to him for guidance. He could not abandon his responsibilities any more than she would stop tending her homestead.

When he showed her how to use the com-tablet, he had shown her vids of Los Angeles from Stalker's reports. If the San Francisco Bay area was anything like LA, some people needed help.

From the intense emotion reflected in his eyes, Falyn could hardly doubt that she was important to him and that he would be back just as he said he would.

"I know it seems far from here on the virtual map display, but not if I transform my sky cycle into flyer mode. I can get here in less than twenty minutes."

"Wow. It would take days to ride my horse that far."

"That would be far too dangerous when you were nearly kidnapped ten miles from here in the middle of nowhere."

"But I feel pretty safe. It's been over a year since anyone showed up here," she said.

"I want you to call me immediately if anyone comes, even if they seem harmless… And carry your pistol when you are outside."

"Is that an order?" she quipped.

Max gave her a quizzical look. "It would be if you were under my command, but it's a request for you. Please be prepared to protect yourself. Will you do that for me?"

"And you be careful out there." She reached for his hand across the table and gave it a gentle squeeze."

All too soon, breakfast was over, and Max kissed her goodbye. It was a deep heartfelt kiss that was no casual leave-taking. It said things neither could yet put into words. Finally, he pulled away from her, running his hand down her arm to grip her hand briefly before he turned and strode out the kitchen door without looking back.

Falyn stood there staring at the kitchen door until she heard the soft whine of his cycle carrying him away. With a deep sigh of acceptance, she went to the row of clothing hooks by the kitchen door and donned her wide-brimmed hat. The food garden needed to be weeded. The auto combine could till the weeds between the rows but not between the plants. She wouldn't be sitting around waiting for Max to come back. There was always work to do on the homestead, and she had best get to it.

Walking out of Falyn's kitchen door to attend to his mission was the hardest thing Max had done in a long time. He almost preferred to be tortured by the Mesaarkans again. Somehow, they'd discovered ways to inflict pain on cyborgs without seriously damaging them. Three days of that had Max wishing to die, but his squad came back for him before it came to that.

Pining for her would not get the job done, which was important. Taking back the second megalopolis from the gangs and their bosses would make it a safer place for Falyn and other women like her who might be mates to his brethren.

With that in mind, Max had studied satellite maps on his internal computer, looking at places with standing structures he could use for his base of operations. He'd found an old prison several miles from the boundary of the megalopolis.

The location showed that most of the buildings seemed to be intact. The Enclave database indicated that the facility had released and abandoned the inmates after the bombings. Otherwise, Max might have found it filled with their remains.

The prison had a nuclear reactor to power it, a useful perk if he could convince the AI to take it off standby and power it up. There were also auxiliary solar collectors and a windmill to pump water from its artesian well.

Satellite records had shown no indication that the facility was occupied. The remote location and the closed gates seemed to support that assumption.

Max arrived there about thirty minutes after leaving Falyn. He stopped his hovercycle inside the fence and lowered his sky cycle in hover mode. He used his internal scanner to check for squatters as he tooled over the roads among the buildings. He found none.

The different buildings represented various levels of security. The first one Max looked inside was filled with cells with bars at the front. Those would be suitable for the gangers, who refused to cooperate. Another building was divided into cubicles with steel doors with small barred windows. They could be used for refugees from the city ruins.

Max was prepared with various means to unlock the doors, but they hadn't been locked when the place was abandoned. After a century of neglect, he was pleased to see the inside was not in bad shape.

The air was stagnant inside, but otherwise, things looked fairly clean. Before the war, they'd been closing prisons in the area. Max processed that this might have been one of them. He found little there that would draw scavengers, and it was fairly remote from the cities, which was why it was still standing.

Now he just needed to find the power plant that pulled the energy resources together to run everything. He sent a message through the cyborg network to the protector units with the coordinates of their new base. Next, he extended his internal sensors seeking the tiniest energy signature which would lead him to the power source.

He found it on the far side of the complex, consisting of thirty buildings. This building was locked, probably because it contained a nuclear reactor. It took Max only seconds to pick the lock with Enclave's handy tools.

Max was surprised that the reactor was not completely shut down but on standby. The AI that ran the system was merely 'sleeping' as he discovered by pinging it. He learned he could get the AI to bring the reactor online, but it told him the batteries for the solar collectors needed to be replaced or rejuvenated.

With the AI set to power up the reactor, Max walked around the compound, exploring the buildings. He was surprised at how much inventory was simply left. He found extra batteries for the solar collectors and determined that the windmill fed electricity through a power converter relay that ran the artesian well pump.

It was getting dark when Max finished his tour of the various buildings. He decided to change out the batteries for the solar collectors to get the lights working and whatever else they supported.

Afterward, he called Falyn to chat for a few minutes and wish her good night. It was bittersweet. While he was happy to see her face and hear her voice, he longed to breed with her again.

Max knew if he went back to her tonight, he would keep her up late, and then he wouldn't be there to do chores while letting her sleep. His own hand would have to do as he replayed their joining from his processors.

Chapter Twelve

"You're still looking for her after all this time?" asked Thorne Driscoll. "Are you sure she's not dead?"

"I don't know anymore. What happened to Tessa started with Devlin White," said Colton. "She promised she would be at the starport when I arrived, and I was on time. She didn't answer my calls or return them. I took a tram to our flat. She hadn't been there for a month, but no one knew where she went."

"By now, she could be offworld, trafficked by one of the other gangs."

"They better hope I never find them! That will be their last day," Colton growled.

"Have you told Thrix what happened in Los Angeles?"

"Yeah, he didn't like it. Have you seen the kid?"

"Eddie? Yeah, he came in yesterday to work, and he's staying at his old hovel."

"Okay, good. I'll com him after I check inventory to make sure someone didn't slip Tessa into one of the holding areas or one of the harems."

"You don't think Thrix would tell you if he had your woman?"

"He might not know he does. But I already went through both the harem and the brothel. I didn't find her," Colton mused. "I don't know where else to look. Anyway, how soon will Gergis get here?"

"End of the month, give or take whether he gets harassed by the Federation."

"He shouldn't. His incoming cargo is absolutely legit. The trick is sending a second shuttle down here and uploading our livestock," Colton said, hiding his distaste.

Despite the fact he'd gone rogue on his undercover assignment, he found selling humans into slavery to aliens abhorrent—especially to Mesaarkans. Colton dealt with Thrix as little as possible since he'd seen the equipment in the alien's little playroom. He didn't want to think about how it was used. Thrix had alluded the equipment was quite versatile.

While he'd had run-ins with the Enclave cyborgs, he wanted them to put Thrix out of business. He'd help if he could, as long as it didn't jeopardize his quest to find Tessa. He'd known Tessa nearly his whole life. They were best friends long before they became lovers and married. No way would she have left when he was on his way home.

Someone took her, and he believed Devlin White orchestrated her abduction. Tessa was exquisitely beautiful and probably valuable for human trafficking. Colton didn't regret killing White; he just didn't care anymore that the Federation knew about it. The sleazy overlord was scum. Colton's only regret was that he didn't suffer enough before he died.

"Gergis better hurry up, Enclave cyborgs are moving in. We may only have half that time to get the merchandise offworld. They will run out all our people and retrieve our stock."

"I will let him know," Driscoll said.

"Do it ASAP. I'm going to find Eddie. See you later." Colton said on his way to the door. "He didn't have much use for Driscoll either. Eddie was the only person he cared about besides Tessa.

Max was outside waiting when five transporters filled with cyborg protectors, equipment, and supplies arrived at the old prison that was now their base. Protector Sergeant was the first to emerge and approach.

"Sergeant Rexas Strong and company reporting for duty." He dipped his head in salute as he came to stand before Max.

Max returned the gesture. "Welcome. This building will be our headquarters and barracks. Each man will have his own room. We'll section off the rest for the refugees we relocate from the ruins and ready more buildings as we need to accommodate them."

"We brought a medical team with us. Do you have a location for sickbay?" Rexas asked.

"That building over there." Max pointed. "A large section served as a medical infirmary. It also has a large mess hall. For now, I want to concentrate on preparing these two buildings for use and equip additional spaces as needed. The Enclave will send auxiliary personnel when we anticipate the refugee's arrival."

"Once the word gets out, we can expect people to come of their own accord," Rexas added. He then relayed how their supplies should be disbursed between the two buildings Max had designated.

"Were you informed that I recently found my genetic mate?"

"I was. Does this mean you will be taking leave?"

"Some, but not extended leave until we get things moving. You will be in charge during my absence, though I will be available through our network and only twenty minutes from here."

"Congratulations, Max. It gives us all hope whenever one of our own finds his mate."

"Plus, our genetic database of females wanting a cyborg mate is expanding. I expect a few to randomly find their mates during our operation here."

While the cyborg protectors unloaded the supplies and their gear into the two buildings, Max and Rexas discussed how they would tackle the city ruins to the west. At the time of the Mesaarkan bombings, the San Francisco

Bay area had grown to a megalopolis that extended east to encompass Sacramento, Stockton, north to Santa Rosa, and south of San Jose.

Areas that were once farmland were gobbled up by the expansion. Homes were carved into the hills with bays and garages for parking hover flyers. It wasn't like the small towns with their own little governments surrounded by rural areas. Max's friend Stalker discovered in Los Angeles that trying to sort out the factions and finding the leaders was inefficient.

Once Stalker figured that out, he'd requested a hundred Protectors to assist in rooting out the gangs and overlords along with the survivors. The quicker they moved them out of the ruins, the sooner they could clear them off and start rebuilding. Some of the overlord's gangers in LA had advanced Mesaarkan weapons that were higher tech than the cyborgs'.

They didn't have internal scanners that could locate the enemy or survivors. No hand-held devices were as quick as the cyborg's internal ones, which fed the info straight into their brains. They could react many times faster than the swiftest human.

As Max and Rexas discussed the strategy for taming the megalopolis, they walked around the huge compound, checking out the buildings for expanding the housing and training of the refugees from the ruins.

"I suggest you start your teams evacuating people from the east side and work your way west. Use explosives to demolish the structures and heavy equipment to clear them."

"That's how I processed the job," said Rexas. "Our heavy equipment should arrive tomorrow along with support personnel to help manage the refugees. Some of them are people Commander Dark's teams rescued five years ago."

"That shows progress. It will take a lot of people to pull this all together. LA and here were probably the densest populated areas in North America before the war," said Max.

"And the bombings left the most people dead in areas like this. No one was prepared for such a massive attack. They broke through all our space fleet defenses and wreaked destruction worldwide."

"Now that I've given you the tour, I'm going to head back to the mountains to spend quality time with my female," Max told him.

"I'd say you earned it, sir. We're glad you warriors returned to Earth and pulled us out of stasis."

"That was Commander Dark's doing, but I am also glad. Com me through our network if anything comes up. I'll be back when I can."

"We've got this, sir. My teams have all been updated with Commander Dark's protocol for evacuation and demolitions," said Rexas.

Max inclined his head in a mini bow salute and headed for his sky cycle. He suppressed the urge to sprint to his vehicle because it might appear unseemly. Even though he was in command of a massive operation, he'd been marking time until he could head back to his mate in the mountains.

He would return as they got deeper into the megalopolis to where the overlord behind the human trafficking could be confronted. Max wanted in on that battle. They were responsible for the attempt to kidnap his Falyn.

Chapter Thirteen

Falyn had just gotten back to the house after chores and set her basket of eggs on the counter when she heard the soft whine of Max's sky cycle. Her first impulse was to run out and throw herself into his arms. Instead, she walked out as he was landing in the yard.

He landed it in the yard about thirty feet away. Climbing off, he covered the distance between them in a few strides and caught her in his arms, lifting her up for a heartfelt, passionate kiss. Falyn met his lips eagerly, wrapping her arms around his neck and her legs around his waist.

While he was gone, part of her feared it was all a dream and he wouldn't return. Because he had never been real.

But he was real. When she was wrapped in his arms, sharing mind-blowing kisses, it felt like he was breathing new life into her soul.

Falyn had gotten used to being alone, keeping busy with chores, and training Angus as he grew. She'd accepted that she would probably die alone on her homestead, and no one would even care.

There were a few people she traded with in town she considered friends, but they were accustomed to seeing her at random intervals. They wouldn't think it odd if she didn't show up for an extended period. Even if it worried them, they wouldn't know where to find her home. She never shared the location with anyone. Strangers could mean trouble.

Falyn had things on her homestead that few people had since the bombings. Her home was powered off the grid. She had a machine to work her garden, water, food, animals, a decent home, and a horse. The isolated location was a blessing and a curse.

Not many people had stumbled onto the homestead. They'd all been friendly and grateful for the hospitality. She had hoped the boy who took her virginity would stay, but she never saw him again when he left.

Falyn half expected it would be the same with Max, but now that she was in his arms, she knew he was real. After he called that morning, she'd planned to make supper for his arrival. Even then, it had still seemed surreal.

The passion in his kisses told her Max was not thinking of food. He wanted her, and she was more than okay with that as desire surged through her body. Her nipples pebbled, aching for his touch, and she could feel the wetness at her core.

Max barely broke the kiss as he carried her to the house and up the back porch steps. Falyn knew exactly where this was going, and she moaned softly in anticipation. In seconds they were inside her bedroom beside her bed, the same bed once shared by her parents. But nothing mattered except that she was in Max's arms where she knew she belonged.

He filled her senses... his kiss, his spicy scent ...her breasts crushed against his chest ...his arms holding her tightly ... his tongue plundering her mouth, staking his claim. She gave it all to him while taking all he offered.

Soon that wasn't enough. Max let her down, and they started pulling off clothes. It took only seconds for them to shed their clothing and come together naked on the bed.

Falyn was eager to have him fill the emptiness between her thighs. But as he lay between her legs, his lips barely an inch from hers, he whispered, "I want to taste you before we breed."

She smiled at him and whispered, "I am all yours...." Caressing his neck and head, raising her head to press her lips to his. She wanted everything, starting with another deep, passionate kiss while his chest pressed down against her sensitive nipples and his cock lay lengthwise against her throbbing clit.

Falyn caressed him wherever she could reach while she let him drag his lips and tongue over her body, kissing and tasting. He spent a long time on her breasts and nipples while she raised her pelvis to rub her clit against his abdomen. That first climax eased her dire need so she could more thoroughly enjoy his foreplay.

She wanted to please him, too. He was taking his own, and she didn't mind. Considering their last time together, Falyn would have many opportunities to return the favor.

She watched as he reached her mons and parted the dark hair over her sex. He drew in a long breath, savoring her musk before he dragged his tongue up her channel and flicked it over her clit.

Letting out a keening moan, she clawed at the bedcover, squirming against Max's hold as he lapped her juices. He continued feasting with his arms around her thighs, holding them apart while anchoring her to the bed. Moaning and panting, she could feel her climax building in her lower belly as her muscles tensed.

As it built, she rubbed her tingling nipples and pinched them as she sensed the need. That sent her over the edge, and she screamed. Trying to buck her hips as shattering waves of ecstasy racked her body. "Omigod, Max!" she cried several times. When her body relaxed, he flicked his tongue across her clit to renew the orgasmic contractions from her uterus, shaking her body.

Falyn knew all the sensations to expect. Her book on human sexuality gave detailed information on human breeding. Only there was no way to convey what it would feel like with Max applying the described technique. She stood the poignant pleasure as long as she could, then finally pushed Max's head, murmuring, "Too sensitive."

Wiping his face with his forearm, he licked her juices off. "You're delicious," he said and moved back on top of her. "Nothing I have ever done compares to the happiness I feel when I am with you."

"I feel that, too," Falyn said, stroking his face with her fingertips. "When I am with you, nothing else matters."

"Take me when you're ready. I want you to have as much pleasure as you give me."

"Believe me, I do." He shifted his hips to find her opening with the tip of his cock. She was so wet that he slid in easily, even with the snug fit. Max lay inside her, briefly, content to kiss her lips and caress her face before he started plunging in and out of her. Once he began, he fucked her long and hard, first on her back facing her, and then from behind. From behind, he could hold her hips and pound into her faster than on top.

Yet it was by no means quick, more like a marathon that wrung out all the pleasure she could take. As Max got close to his orgasm, he reached around and pinched her clit. She wailed as her orgasm crashed through her, sending him roaring into his. Feeling his hot semen shooting into her womb made her come even harder.

It was magnificent, though it sapped nearly every last bit of energy from her body. It felt so good...

Both completely sated, he pulled out and lay beside her, pulling her into his arms, kissing her lips tenderly. Falyn felt utterly boneless and sleepy and wonderful.

She spoke his name as an endearment and caressed his cheek. "I'm so glad you're back."

"So, am I. Believe me, it was hard to stay away and do my job. But I have the chief protector in charge, and he knows what to do."

"How long before you have to go back?"

"At least three weeks," he assured her. "Bonding with my genetic mate is too distracting for me to concentrate on doing my job when all I want to do is breed with you."

"Is that all you want?"

"Of course, not all... I want to be at your side... and take care of you. I want to know everything about you. Most of all, I want to be with you when we're not breeding, but I will always want you that way, too. I served my whole life fighting a war so I could finally have someone to love who would love me back and maybe someday make offspring together."

"I always figured I would never have that, living way out here. There was one boy years ago, I thought maybe.... But he left, and I never saw him again. Some guys in town made lewd offers, but I knew they just wanted to get laid. They were nobody I wanted in my life. I knew right away you were different. Right now, I don't know that I love you; I just know that I want to be with you. Mom said that love happens over time, but more often than not, lust brings people together. Love is what makes them stay together."

"Falyn, know that I am here to stay. I will do the job I agreed on, but the rest of my time is   yours."

Chapter Fourteen

Colton found his asset Eddie Hill in his hovel, kicked back on his pallet, playing a game on his com-tablet.

"Hey, kid. Do you think you should pay better attention to who's walking in your door? If I came here to kill you, you're already dead."

"Except my little fly cam sent your image to my tablet as you approached. Since I'm still breathing, you must not be here to kill me," Eddie said. "Glad to see you made it back."

Colton shook his head as he sat on an old plastic crate. "I made it back, but I couldn't get the Mesaarkan flyer back from Cyborg Ranger Stalker."

"Was Thrix pissed?"

"He didn't even ask, and I didn't offer the info. We've got bigger problems. The Enclave is taking over this city. They just brought in a hundred cyborgs with more on the way."

"They're going to take down Thrix's operation just like they did in LA. His gangers are not going to stop them. The high-tech weapons Thrix promised are coming in with Gergis. I think they will hit Thrix before Gergis ever gets here." Colton shuffled toward Eddie, pushing obstacles out of his path with his booted foot.

Eddie had paused his game to give Colton his full attention. "I thought you said we had more time."

"We did until Enclave sent another ranger to work San Francisco megalopolis. We're down to weeks. They could get here before Gergis. If they catch you, you'll end up either at their refugee camp or headed for the prison planet."

"What about you?"

"I have to make sure none of the females they are selling is Tessa."

"Then what?"

"My cabin is in the mountains of the eastern overlord territory. I plan to go back there when I find Tessa."

"What if you never do?"

"It's not an option. I'm not giving up."

"So, what am I supposed to do?" asked Eddie.

"Get out of this business altogether. When they start sweeping the ruins to evacuate people before demolition, get yourself evacuated. The Enclave will give you a homestead, and you can have a fresh start. They don't have to know you were in on this."

"What do I know about homesteading?"

"You're young and smart. You can learn. They will help you. What else is there? Would you rather go to prison?"

"Fuck, no."

"Then, do what I tell you. You're on the losing side if you don't."

"You're not one of us, are you?" Eddie, met his gaze accusingly.

Colton didn't look away. "That doesn't matter. I'm your friend. I never lied to you, and I won't start now. You can have a good life. Find a female, start a family. There's no future in this business. You will either go to prison, or end up dead. I don't want that for you."

"Will I ever see you again?"

Colton shrugged. "It could happen."

A moment later, he was gone. Eddie had a lot to think about.

Dawn was breaking as Max stood sipping a mug of tea on the back porch of the home he now shared with Falyn. He'd seen many sunrises and sunsets while fighting the war with his brethren on many different planets. Nowhere in the galaxy had he felt more at peace, secure in knowing he was where he was meant to be.

Falyn was still sleeping, "delightfully exhausted," as she'd put it, from making love—breeding until the wee hours. She'd fallen asleep in his arms with her head on his upper chest naked. He had drifted asleep, remembering every kiss, every touch, and the sheer joy of sliding his cock into her that first thrust.

He didn't mind that she required hours more sleep than he did. The alone time allowed him to contemplate his new life living in the quiet beauty of these mountains with Falyn.

It also gave him time to check in with Rexas on their evacuation and demolition plan progress. As in LA, many buildings still partly intact held only the remains of long-dead residents. Rexas's team evacuated a few hundred from the ruins in the first week.

Some had to be forcibly removed, terrified they would be sold into slavery. Many had been chased by gangers, hunting for humans to sell. Converted cyborg naturals were among the gangers helping and commanding them. They didn't know the difference between the converted naturally born humans and the manufactured cyborgs.

Rexas calmed them as much as possible once they got to the base. Distributing meal trays in the mess hall helped pacify them while his second in command explained why they were there. The social transition counselors arrived two days later.

Max was fully satisfied with how Rexas was handling the job. So far, they hadn't encountered many gangers or evidence that any residents possessed high-tech weapons. They mostly showed up with projectile guns, crossbows, longbows, knives, and swords. None of those would penetrate the cyborgs' armor. They might stab or cut a cyborg not wearing armor, but it took real strength to penetrate their flesh deeply with an ordinary knife or sword.

The cleanup crews and heavy machinery arrived a week after the protectors. Two weeks into the job, things were going as they should. The low point was finding so many remains of long-dead residents everywhere they cleared.

Recon teams located most of the gang-held overlord territory. They were holding areas close to the bay. It would be a while before they got close because the teams were running evacuations and demolitions north and south. Max chose that strategy so he could spend more time with Falyn.

Finishing his tea, Max returned the mug to the kitchen and went back outside to do morning chores. He let out the horses, milked the goats, fed the chickens, and collected eggs. He'd already weeded the garden two days earlier.

Max and Falyn did evening chores together and picked any fruits and vegetables ready for use the next day. Only today they would harvest produce to trade in the town.

"You really don't need to do this anymore, Falyn," he told her during dinner yesterday. "I can get you the things you need. I have most of the credits I ever earned during the war."

Falyn gave him an indulgent smile. "It's sweet of you to offer, but the people I trade with depend on the food I bring them. Anyway, you got the grain for the horses. That's a big help. Besides, it will allow you to meet them and tell them about the Enclave. They would surely appreciate getting com-tablets like the one you gave me."

"I should probably go down to the base and pick up a case of them to distribute," he told her. "We could drop off the produce and sky cycle down to the base to pick them up. You can see my base of operations."

"You mean to fly?"

"Yes."

"I don't know if I can do that. Going up that high in the sky scares me more than a little."

"Do you trust me?"

"Yes, but…."

"My sky cycle is safe. I've flown it across the country and back. Not a single one has crashed due to any failure of the vehicle. The only one that crashed was shot down by a hostile."

She gave him a torn look.

"Falyn…" Max reached for her hand across the table and brought it to his lips. "I'm not going to let anything happen to you. You are the mate I've waited my whole life to find."

She met his gaze steadily, and Max could see her fighting back her fear. "It's much faster to fly than to hover close to the ground. We could leave after morning chores and be back in time for evening chores."

"I know that people flew all the time before the war. I read about it in some of our old books and magazines." She paused, closed her eyes, took a breath, and let it out. Meeting his gaze again, she nodded. "Okay. But I'm still scared."

Max smiled to himself as he finished the chores. She was scared, but she was still going to fly with him. That made her brave in his eyes.

He heard a sound that made him look up as he strolled back to the house with the egg basket. Falyn was standing on the back porch wearing only a thin, cream-colored robe and nothing else. It gapped open to the belt at her waist in a deep vee.

Max went hard almost immediately.

Falyn stepped onto the porch to see Max strolling toward the house as though he hadn't a care in the world. She was sure he'd gone to do chores when she awoke alone in bed. During the war, cyborgs went weeks at a time without sleep, sometimes longer. So, when he woke early, he did morning chores.

Ever since he arrived in the middle of her life, she had yearned to fuck him. She didn't know whether she was making up for lost time; or if the pheromones fueled her desire.

Falyn had started meeting him as he returned from chores wearing only the thin robe and nothing else. She thought nothing of stepping outside dressed like that because it had been years since anyone approached her house.

His dark, smoldering look told her she would get what she wanted. He stalked up the four steps and set the basket of eggs on the little table beside the back door. Falyn stared up at him as he backed her against the wall.

She knew he could scent her arousal as she stared up at him, mesmerized. Pushing the sides of her robe further apart, he plucked at her taut nipples, then kneaded her breasts.

Max lifted her up, pressing her against the wall, leaning into her. Falyn wrapped her arms and legs around him, still holding his gaze.

"Max." She whispered his name just before he claimed her lips in a deep, sensual kiss. He slid his hands between them, using his body to balance her against the wall, and flicked his thumbs back and forth over her nipples until she was moaning and squirming.

Still kissing her, he ripped open the hook-loop closure on his cargo pants and let them drop. He gripped her buttocks and found her opening, sliding his cock into her wet heat.

Falyn groaned at the exquisite pleasure his filling her with his cock brought her.

"Is this what you want?" Max asked in a sexy growl as he broke from the kiss, thrusting hard into her.

"Y-yes," her breath hitched at the profound pleasure as he hit all the right spots. Then his mouth was on hers again as he drove his cock into her hard and deep.

Soon he was pounding into her while Falyn clung to his shoulders. Max was careful to hold her, so she didn't slam into the wall while he fucked her. She cried out with the first two orgasms and screamed on the third when Max found his.

"Mm, Max, you are so good!" she laughed softly, caressing his face. He may have been shy in the beginning, but not anymore. As she kissed and ran her hands over him, she realized how happy she was to have him in her life.

Chapter Fifteen

By the time they'd showered and eaten breakfast, it was almost midday. They'd found a plastic box that fit atop the cargo compartment to carry the vegetables Falyn insisted on taking to town.

Max didn't mind indulging her. He adored her and would do anything he could to make her happy. While they enjoyed powerful sexual chemistry, he also enjoyed just being with her in the moment.

Falyn's nervousness about flying for the first time in her life was evident, yet she appeared determined to conquer her fear. The fifteen miles to town would be a five-minute flight. At varying speeds with stretches of rough terrain, riding Angus would take at least a couple hours, and they didn't have a horse that could carry a cyborg's weight for Max.

He would easily keep up on foot, but it wasn't the same. Max was seriously thinking about getting a horse after discussing it with Captain Blaze Savage. The head of the cyborg ranger team found he enjoyed the kinship he'd found with his own horse. So, Max made inquiries over the AI net to find a large, strong draft horse.

Meanwhile, he directed Falyn to sit on the passenger seat, then swung his leg over the handlebar to sit in the driver's seat. Falyn was only too happy to wrap her arms around Max and hold him tightly, her cheek pressed to his broad back as he sent his bike into a vertical ascent.

He morphed the hybrid vehicle at several hundred feet into a flyer with a fully enclosed cockpit.

Falyn looked out over the landscape through a port window. Although she knew she was in the air, it didn't seem so frightening with her arms wrapped around Max.

"Ready?"

"Yes," she assured him, but she knew Max could easily tell she was still scared by the rapid rhythm of her heart. "Ready as I will ever be," she added resignedly. If she was going to die, her last memory would be of holding the man she *loved.*

Falyn sucked in a startled breath, realizing the significance of the thought that just popped into her head unbidden. She loved Max! It hadn't been that long, yet she knew it was true. Smiling, she hugged Max more tightly as he set the craft into forward motion.

Rather than shooting down the mountainscape at high speed, he let the craft glide slowly over the tree tops. "This isn't so bad," Falyn admitted as she noticed. "It just feels like we are floating."

"It's slower than I usually travel, but I decided to ease you into it. We will get there in ten minutes instead of five."

They touched down in Marcus Flats exactly ten minutes after leaving Falyn's homestead. The town had one main street with side streets branching off it. Houses were spaced apart comfortably so that neighbors didn't look into each other's windows.

Falyn directed Max to the weaver's house for their first stop. The weaver had a modest one-story home on a two-acre lot with one acre planted in cotton. Falyn had brought some bar soap, vegetables, and goat cheese for clothing she had already gotten. Max accompanied her when she went to the door to knock.

The older woman was slightly startled when she saw all 6'6" Max's powerfully built form in his t-shirt, cargo pants, and ranger hat with the circled star emblem.

"Hi Millie, I brought you the goods I promised." She held up a cloth bag. "First, let me introduce my mate, Max Steele. He's a Federation cyborg ranger. Max, this is my friend Millie Fox."

"Well, this is a surprise! When did this happen?" Millie opened the screen door. "Come on in and tell me all about it."

Once inside, Falyn handed off the cloth bag to Millie, and Millie directed them to sit on the rustic padded sofa in her spacious living room. The room was divided into a sitting area and Millie's work area. There were two different-sized looms and a spinning wheel with a basket of cotton beside it.

"I'll be right back," Millie said, heading for the kitchen. "Can I get you two anything to drink?"

Falyn looked to Max, who shook his head. "No, thanks, Millie. We just ate breakfast. We're fine."

Their hostess returned to the room, returning the empty cloth bag to Falyn. "So, Mr. Steele, what brings you to these parts?"

"The Civil Restoration Enclave of North America is re-establishing law and order in most of North America. The project's second stage is to restore the infrastructure needed to bring the standard of living up to pre-war levels. Right now, I have teams working on the San Francisco Bay area megalopolis."

"Does that mean they are taking over?"

"Not at all. Do you have a mayor or a town leader?"

"We do, Kevin Gray. He just lives down the road from here. We elected him two years ago, and our town council---four people."

"Any police or law enforcer?"

"We haven't needed anyone until those four from out of town showed up trying to kidnap young women and boys."

"Well, they won't be bothering people here anymore. Max caught them and sent them off to jail," Falyn told her proudly. She continued telling how they met, the shooting, and how Max repaired her horse's broken leg.

Millie chuckled. "I can see why you fell for this guy. He's definitely a keeper."

"Oh, Millie, it's not funny. I felt terrible when the gun went off. When I saw the blood where the bullet hit, I thought I'd killed him."

"How are you still with us?" asked Millie.

"Cyborgs have metal alloy skeletons, including my sternum. That stopped the bullet," Max explained. "I knew it was accidental."

"Falyn is much too nice to shoot someone on purpose. She cries when she has to kill a chicken to put food on her table."

Max just smiled to himself. He had already discovered how tender and caring his mate was.

"Back to the Enclave and your local government... If you have a town government, they will represent your town to the Enclave. They have gone back to the original Constitution of the United States with some revisions to cover our level of technology and the state of civilization.

"Falyn and I are going to my base to pick up com-tablets that will allow you to communicate with the Enclave and access the AI net for news, information, and entertainment archives."

"I'm not sure I would even know how to use something like that."

"Easy as pie," said Falyn. "You can just tell it what to do. Even turn it on by voice command. Max got me one, and I learned to use it right away. That means you can call me when you're running low or have one of my orders ready."

"Now, that would be really handy."

"Since cargo space is limited on my sky cycle, we will probably bring back twenty-five this run. We'll give you one and see the mayor about distributing one to each family. We can have a drone drop deliver more if needed." Max explained and turned to Falyn. "Is there anything else you need to discuss with Millie?"

Falyn thought for a moment and shook her head. "We should go if we expect to get back in time for chores."

"Yes. If you two think of anything else, you can chat when we bring back the tablets." Max stood, then Falyn and Millie stood as well.

The two women hugged, indicating clearly to Max that they cared for each other deeply.

Since Mayor Kevin Gray's house was only two houses down, Max and Falyn walked. Falyn also knew him and his wife fairly well. They traded seeds for food crops and grain.

Mayor Gray was in his garden picking squash when they arrived. As he stood to his full height, he was only a few inches shorter than Max but with a slender, wiry build. He wore a short dark beard, with shoulder-length hair tied with a leather string at the nape of his neck.

"Hello, Falyn. This is a pleasant surprise. What brings you to Marcus Flats? And you brought company." Kevin nodded to Max, assessing the other man briefly before turning his attention back to Falyn.

She made introductions and reviewed the information they'd given Millie just a few minutes earlier. Kevin was both intrigued and interested, including that there were cyborgs in the territory looking for genetic mates. The mayor of Marcus had four grown daughters of mating age, and there were slim pickings of suitable males in the town and the surrounding area.

"Once you have your com-tablet, you can contact the cyborg genetic matching service to enter your daughters into the database. Perhaps they will match some of the thousands of cyborgs in our database looking for mates."

"How long will that take?"

"Once we get a tech to you for the scan, you should hear back in a day or two. They will be notified with an attached video if their matches are found. The cyborg will not be notified unless your daughter approves."

"And you say that genetics is the only criteria?"

"Each cyborg is engineered to respond only to a female with specific genetics, and she is the only female with whom he can mate and have children."

"Well, doesn't that just beat all?" Kevin said, smiling in amazement.

As Max and Falyn walked back to his sky cycle, Max said, "It's really nice to come to a place where people are actually glad to see me instead of shooting at me."

Falyn laughed ironically because she was one of those people, glad Max wasn't holding it against her.

Chapter Sixteen

"They're coming tomorrow," said ganger looking back at Colton from his com-tablet.

He was one of the gangers who'd infiltrated the ruins to get into the cyborg base. Lander was his name. He'd been hanging around eavesdropping wherever he could.

The cyborgs naturally shared information over their exclusive internal network, but had started to share orally as they became integrated with humans. They didn't see any threat in the humans they rescued from the ruins.

Colton didn't fault their logic. Most of those people were harmless. Thrix wanted intel; Colton made it happen. Even with the Mesaarkan tech, they didn't have enough manpower and arms to hold off a hundred cyborgs with heavy armor and weapons. They would have to bug out.

Thrix would probably lose his collection of humans for shipment to the slave auctions. Colton Price didn't care about that. Unless he found Tessa first, he would sign on with Gergis and go to the auction houses to hack the sales records for clues to where she was sold. He would never give up until he found her or her remains.

No one would convince him that she left days before he was due back to reunite with her. They loved each other too much for that. Not once did Tessa waver in her enthusiasm for his homecoming. She had been marking off the days for three months.

All that aside, the devotion in her eyes never wavered. Nor had his. He only signed up for war to help fend off the invasion of Earth two years before the peace treaty was ratified. A year and a half later, he'd suffered catastrophic injuries that took him out of the fight. To save his life, they made him a cyborg.

When he came to terms with it and contacted Tessa, the treaty was signed, and the war was over. Colton told her how he'd been changed in case she couldn't accept his physical changes.

"Colton Price! After all these years, you should know me better than that. I love you, and that's never going to change. I don't care if they replaced some of your parts with cybernetics. You still have two arms and two legs. You still have your dick…."

That had made him laugh. "What if I didn't?"

"You still have your lips and tongue. You have hands. We would figure something out."

That gave him another chuckle. "I love you, Tessa, and I can't wait to show you how well all my parts are working, especially my dick."

"Ooh, you're making me wet just thinking about it," she confessed.

Yeah, it made his cock hard, too. That was the last time Colton had heard from her. When all his subsequent calls went unanswered, he knew something was wrong. Something happened that she couldn't answer.

He squeezed his eyes shut as they filled with unshed tears. If Tessa was dead, so was everyone responsible. He would learn the truth if it was the last thing he ever did.

Breeding once with Falyn was never enough. Max's enhancements included the ability to quickly regain his erection after ejaculation. He thoroughly relished her unabashed pleasure in their mating. She would keen and sob and hum her delight in fucking him.

She raised her pelvis to meet his thrust for thrust hugging his cock with her inner walls, watching his face as he watched hers. He felt like they were part of each other, and loving her finally made him whole. Part of him longed for her to say the words. But did he really need her to speak them?

Falyn had already accepted him into her home and her life. She made him feel as though he belonged and thought he was important to her.

He felt his orgasm coiling low in his back while he sensed Falyn tensing as she was getting close. She made a few short sobbing sounds and one long 'ah' as her body shuddered with orgasm. "Ah, Max. Oh, Max," she cried out as he filled her with his semen; she came even harder. She dug her short nails into his back in ecstasy, and the slight sting enhanced his pleasure.

When she had milked him of every drop and lay quietly beneath him, still joined, and she held him tightly, he kissed her soft lips with all the tenderness he felt for her. Falyn kissed him back with the same reverence, caressing his back and head.

Pulling part way out of her and thrusting back into her, he set off a new orgasmic wave of contractions around his cock. Falyn smiled up at him, caressing his face. Looking straight into his midnight blue eyes, she said, "Max, I love you."

Max looked at her for a stunning moment and smiled. "I love you, too… from the moment I knew you were mine."

They remain joined for several more minutes, kissing and caressing in orgasmic bliss. Max finally pulled out of her and rolled them on their sides. Falyn was getting sleepy after two long hard rounds of breeding. He held her until she drifted to sleep which didn't take long.

Slipping carefully out of bed, so he didn't wake her, Max went to the bathroom to clean up. Retrieving his clothing from the floor, he dressed and headed outside to take care of the animals and collect the eggs.

When Falyn shuffled out into the kitchen after a two-hour nap, Max made omelets with veggies and goat cheese, with a pot of herbal tea steeping on the counter. She was barefoot, wearing only her robe belted at the waist, and her hair, still damp from the shower, was neatly combed.

"Oh, Max, that is so sweet of you. I was just getting up to make us something to eat."

He set down the cast iron frying pan and gathered her in his arms, pulling her against him. "I don't mind at all, Falyn. I would do anything for you."

Falyn slid her arms around his waist and pressed her cheek against his chest. She knew he had an ulterior motive. He was ensuring she rested for more sex after dinner... not that she opposed the idea.

They were taking on the overlord tomorrow and rooting out as many gangers as possible. Max didn't seem worried, but she was a little concerned. Mesaarkans were involved in human trafficking. They could have weapons; the cyborgs didn't expect.

"Hey, don't worry," Max soothed. "I will be fine. I know how to fight Mesaarkans. We're not even sure there are any here. None of the gangers we interrogated have ever seen any. They only mentioned the cyborg Colton and a middleman called Driscoll."

"What about all the other overlords?"

"We'll get them. We can't let them transport the abductees off-world first. That is our primary objective whether we get the overlord and the gangers." He paused, pressing a kiss to the top of her head. "Be glad this is not the war. It would be Captain Savage and the other five of us going on this mission alone."

Falyn refused to ask him not to go, even though that's exactly what she wanted. Now that she had opened her life and made him part of it, she couldn't entirely quash the fear that he might not return. Then everything would go back to how it was before he flew into her life on his sky cycle.

Max frowned as she looked up at him, and she knew he'd seen her doubt. "Falyn, don't even think it. I am your male. I would die for you, but I will never leave you as long as I live. I've fought my way out of far worse than what we are facing tomorrow."

Falyn nodded, meeting his gaze, and he lowered his head to claim her lips in a passionate kiss. "Now, let's eat before it gets cold," he said when he parted his lips from hers.

When they were seated at the table, Max watched Falyn take her first bite and waited.

"Mm, this is so good!" she assured him.

Max gave her a warm smile as she continued eating. "One of the millions of recipes on the AI network. I put in the ingredients on hand, and it returned several recipes. I will save this one."

"You are getting pretty good at cooking. Didn't you have food processors that would fabricate any meal you wanted?"

"Only on the ship and at the bases. We had to improvise when we were on a mission and ran out of meal bars. We hunted for meat and edibles. Sometimes we ate bugs and grubs to survive."

"I never got a processor while I was on Phantom. I found I liked preparing food from scratch. Some of the other cyborgs liked growing things and raising livestock. I like to fix things, so we traded food for labor."

"That sounds nice."

Max shrugged. "We were killing time until we could find our genetic mates. But now that I have, I'm glad I learned to cook so I can cook for you."

Falyn could see that he meant every word. She didn't know what to say, so she smiled at him, deeply touched by his thoughtfulness and devotion.

After breakfast, Max got out his spare ion rifle, and took Falyn outside to the field to show her how to use it. He hung some pieces of firewood from tree branches at the edge of the woods to shoot. He went through all the settings and safety procedures and had her repeat it all back to him.

"Now, you don't have to worry about the kick back. It's much less than your shotgun," Max explained and handed her the weapon. "There are your targets."

Her first try, she only hit two out of six, but took out a couple four-inch trees. Her next attempt took two of four, and another try hit the other two.

"Okay, now set it on repeat and aim at the ground in front of the tree line and use a sweeping motion across your target."

Following his instructions, the rifle dug a small channel in the dirt without damaging any trees. Next, he went through all the instructions on how to use a blaster, telling her not to let the enemy get that close. After she shot it several times, she holstered it.

"Use the rifle on intruders." He asserted. "Call me if anyone comes, especially if they say I sent them."

"Yes, sir," Falyn teased, giving him an old-fashioned salute.

Max gave her an indulgent smile, shouldered the rifle, and pulled her against him, hugging her. He felt torn between fear for his mate and his duty to his job, then reminded himself that she had survived alone for eight years without anyone to care for her.

Still, leaving her would be so hard.

Chapter Seventeen

Max slowed the sky cycle when they neared his base of operations and retracted the cockpit cover so Falyn could get the full effect of the sky view.

"I found this on a satellite map. It's just outside the perimeter of the Mesaarkans bomb range. All of the buildings are in good repair, and the complex has its own power plant," Max explained.

"It's huge!" Falyn exclaimed. "What is this place?"

"It used to be a prison. I needed a place where people from the ruins could live while Enclave teams clear away the rubble and build new homes for them. Then we have the one-hundred protectors, medical personnel, counselors, and educators. Some of the protectors have mates, and we also have some gangers as prisoners. As we get closer to the overlord's stronghold, there will be more of those."

"Wow, this is practically a whole town."

"That's what we need. The protectors have found more people than we expected living in the ruins. I'm not sure why."

"Maybe more people escaped the other megalopolis and went out into the country. Or maybe more died in the initial bombings," Falyn suggested.

"It's going to be a month before the first houses are ready for them, and we won't know how many we need until we evacuate the sites for demolition and reclaiming."

Max brought the sky cycle to land in front of one of the larger buildings. "We're using this building for our headquarters and main barracks for our cyborg personnel. Then the building over there is for the rotating Enclave workers." Max pointed to a building directly across from the barracks.

"The building we need is the next one over." He gestured toward another large one-story building to the left of the barracks. With his hand at the small of her back, he guided her at his side toward the building.

"This building has the mess hall and the infirmary plus stores."

In the distance, Falyn could see children playing by the rescue barracks with a few adults watching them. "Max, how will these people function on their own once you've put them into new houses?"

"The Enclave sent educators already holding classes for them on their new homes and growing their own food. It's amazing that so many survived the living conditions."

The demolitions crew found hundreds of skeletal, human remains in dwellings where they died on the day of the bombings. Falyn had seen vids of Chicago when Vyken Dark and his teams arrived five years before. That was as close as Max wanted Falyn to get to any of it.

Max signed out a case of com-tablets for the people of Marcus Flats. They met Rexas, his second in command, as they were leaving the building. Rexas nodded in salute. They communicated over the cyborg net at least once a day, so there was nothing they needed to discuss. "Rexas, I would like to introduce you to my mate Falyn Wayne. Falyn, my second Rexas Strong."

"Pleased to meet you," she replied with a shy smile.

Rexas dipped his head politely. "I am honored." Then to Max, he said, "we will be ready in two days to move on the Thrix territory."

"I'll be back tomorrow to resume my duties. Unless something changes, we'll use the plan we made based on your intel."

"We didn't learn when the abductees will be transported because we can't project when the slave ship will arrive."

"But you have their locations?"

"Yes, and we have men patrolling the area in shifts. The slave ship will come in cloaked, so *Starfire Nemesis* most likely won't be able to intercept."

"What's the latest estimate on the captives?"

"We scanned seventy-three in the holding structure, but some could be gangers. We'll sort them out when we've secured them." Rexas assured him. That's all I have, sir."

"Thanks for the update; I will see you tomorrow." Max nodded and headed for his cycle carrying the box of foldable com-tablets.

Falyn sighed as she walked beside him. "I guess that means I won't have you all to myself anymore."

They reached the cycle and opened the cargo compartment. There was just enough room to fit the box. "I plan to be home almost every night in time for evening chores so you can save your energy for breeding."

Falyn chuckled. "In that case, I guess I can live with that." She was obviously flirting with him, and he loved it.

It seemed like more than three weeks since he found her about to shoot her injured horse. They had bonded as much over running the homestead as they had during sex. He only wanted her almost every waking moment of every day.

As soon as the box of com-tablets was secure, they got back on and headed up the mountain. Max took them to a height over the treetops and extended the wings to go twice the speed he could hover over the ground.

They returned to Millie's house first and gave her the first tablet and a quick lesson on how to use it. Although all relevant active codes would be available through the satellite network, Falyn gave Millie her code to make it easier for her to get in touch.

They took the rest to Mayor Kevin Gray to distribute. "For now, we are issuing one to a household. If you have extra, dole them out to people who benefit the community," Max told him."

"Thank you, Ranger." To Falyn, he said, "Looks like you got yourself a fine young man. It's not good for a beautiful young woman to live alone in the mountains."

"You know I got by," said Falyn. "But he is sure nice to have around." She smiled and winked at Max and headed for the sky cycle.

Max frowned at Kevin's words, reminding him that Falyn would be alone at the homestead while he was at work. He shook his head as he followed her to the bike. He mentally shook himself. There was no reason to believe there would be problems. No one knew where her home was located.

He decided to ride over the homestead to scan for any nearby people. The closest human he found was a man living in a cabin ten miles from the homestead. Falyn knew of him, but they had never met. Everywhere else was clear.

Only Rexas and Cyborg Command at the Enclave base had the coordinates of the homestead. He didn't forget Captain Savage's home was blown up and his wife taken. So far, he hadn't pissed off the wrong people like Savage had.

However, just in case, he would show Falyn how to use his extra ion rifle in the morning before he left. She didn't have to be a good shot with that on automatic. It could kill a dozen enemies in one sweep.

Once he'd formed the plan. He put it out of his mind, calculating whether they had time for a breeding session before chores. If so, he would end up doing them alone, but it was worth it. He smiled to himself as they headed for home. Just thinking of breeding with his beautiful mate made his cock stiffen.

As soon as they got inside the kitchen at the house, they were in each other's arms, kissing in a burning flare of desire. Max lifted Falyn for her to wrap her legs around him, cupping her buttocks as he kissed her deeply with his tongue, teasing and caressing hers.

Max had scented her desire all the way home, making their joining all the more urgent. Inside their shared bedroom, he had them both stripped naked in seconds. Her pussy already slick for him, she crawled onto the bed on all fours offering Max access from behind.

They both groaned in bliss as Max slid his cock deep into her and fingered her clit. Leaning over her, he put his forearm across her sensitive breasts and massaged them.

"Ah, Max," she purred, and he nuzzled her neck. "You're the best…."

Then she gasped as he drew back and thrust into her hard, pressing on her clit and squeezing her breasts with his arms. He did that a few more times before she came, keening her delight as her inner walls clamped down on his cock.

Max loved that he could do that to her, that she was so responsive and receptive to his lovemaking. She always made him feel so good, especially when she initiated their breeding. He pressed her clit and thrust into her intermittently, teasing her through her orgasm before he took his own pleasure, pounding into her.

Falyn left no doubt in his mind that he pleased her and himself. She would egg him on with her wails and cries. "God, yes, fuck me hard. Yes, yes! I am yours. Oh, fuck!"

Yes, he would be doing the chores while Falyn recovered, and he didn't mind. She was so worth it.

Chapter Eighteen

Colton was frustrated that he couldn't find any leads on what happened to Tessa. He wondered whether the Enclave cyborgs had picked her up in their sweeps of the ruins before demolition.

He couldn't go ask them after he tried to kill Stalker back in L.A. But maybe Driscoll's ganger plant inside their base could check for him. Colton had dozens of pictures stored in his internal CPU. He even had that last exchange with her telling him she still loved him and wanted him to come home. He played it nearly every single day, sometimes more than once.

He just couldn't give up until he knew for certain that she was dead. And Colton wouldn't let himself believe that without indisputable proof. That's why he was on his way to see Driscoll. He didn't have Lander's contact info, so he wanted Driscoll to make contact with him.

Driscoll operated from the single building on the block untouched in the bombings save for a few broken windows. One of those broken windows allowed him to eavesdrop as he approached.

"Thanks, Lander. We'll be ready for them. I got the coordinates for the female's homestead. Call me immediately when they leave the base, and I will send a team after her. Once we have her, he won't interfere."

"Then what?"

"I will send her with Gergis, and he will never see her again. Then he will be useless to the Enclave. He will regret trying to take what's ours."

Colton had no love for the manufactured cyborgs, but he had no love for Driscoll either. Taking Max's female didn't sit well with him at all. He may have gone rogue, but he still planned to fulfill his mission.

He would just do it his way.

Max held Falyn one last time before he left for the mission. Despite a slow and thorough lovemaking session before breakfast and again after shooting practice, he still wanted her again. She held him tightly, pressing her cheek into the hollow of his shoulder.

"Don't worry, sweetling. I won't be away one moment longer than I need to. And remember to keep that ion rifle in easy reach whenever you are outside or anywhere."

"I will," she murmured and looked up at him. "I'm okay. I lived here alone for quite a while before you came. I can certainly manage for a few hours or even days. But I will miss you." She said the last with a smile.

Max smiled back at her and then kissed her parted lips. Falyn suspected he'd intended a light kiss before he headed out, but it took a lot longer and ended with them both aroused.

"We'll continue this when you get back," Falyn assured him. "I love you. Stay safe."

"I love you, too. Com me if you have any problems." Max let her go and turned resolutely, heading out the door without looking back.

Falyn waited until she heard the sky cycle take off before she gathered up the ion rifle and headed out to the barn to milk the goats. She was glad to have enough chores to last the whole day. It would make the time go faster until Max returned.

Max's assault teams were ready to go when he arrived at the base. They had found the barracks where the gangers were holding the abductees. The building was located a klick from the heart of the chief overlord's territory.

The cyborgs brought four large hovercrafts to evacuate the abductees to the base before they went after the gangers. By the number of gangers firing on them as they approached the target, Max knew they expected them.

That could only mean they had an overlord spy among the rescues from the ruins. Likely one of the gangers who "surrendered" for a chance at a better life.

It didn't matter. Despite rumors of Mesaarkan tech, these enforcers had only conventional projectile weapons with a few blasters. None of that would faze fully armored cyborgs with ion rifles and military blasters. Max's teams could have easily killed the gangers in a short time, but the Enclave wanted them taken alive for re-education.

They managed to capture about seventy percent of them and bound their hands and feet with zip ties while they were still unconscious. A few protectors stood guard by the prisoners, and others secured the perimeter around the barracks.

Max planned to go to the first barracks with Rexas to assess the abductees when his com beeped. He receded his armor to take it from an inside pocket. Expecting it to be Falyn, he was surprised to see Colton Price on his screen.

"Price, what the fuck do you want?"

"That's Agent Price to you, Ranger. You'll want to hear what I have to tell you." He paused for effect.

"I am in the middle of a mission and don't have time to chat."

"Driscoll sent a team to capture your mate. He figures he can hold you off until the slave ship comes for the captives. Then he will put her on the ship with the rest of them."

"And why should I believe you?"

"Look, Steele, I may have gone a little rogue on this assignment, but we're still on the same side. Man, they took my wife; I don't want that to happen to anyone else."

"I'll look into it." Max had no sooner ended the call than his com beeped. It was Falyn.

"Max, there are men here. They came in a flyer, and I don't know what they want."

"Where are you now?" Max ran for his sky cycle.

"I'm in the house in the upstairs bedroom over the kitchen. I locked all the doors."

"I'm on my way. Can you hold them off?"

"I've got the rifle. I think so. They're coming toward the house. I got to go…."

Max climbed on his cycle and took off vertically while converting to flyer mode. He sent a message to his second in command, who was more than capable of handling the situation. As he jetted off toward home, he noted that Falyn never ended the transmission. Max transferred it to his internal computer so he could detect what was happening at her end.

It seemed like the longest ten minutes of his life.

Falyn dropped the com-tablet on the single bed by the window. Four men climbed out of the flyer parked in the pasture and strode purposefully toward her house. At least two of them were armed, but she couldn't tell what kind of guns they had.

She'd been taking a break with some cold tea in the kitchen after weeding the garden when she heard a flyer coming to land. It was a deeper, more robust sound than Max's Skycycle. As it settled in the horse pasture, Falyn locked the kitchen door and grabbed the ion rifle beside it.

Running to the living room, she locked that door as well, then ran upstairs to her old room to the window that overlooked the pasture. Four males came out of the vehicle, ducking under the butterfly doors. Sighting them through the rifle scope, she saw they were all armed with automatic long guns.

Rounding the single bed behind her, she lifted it on its side and pushed it against the wall under the window. Her com-tablet clattered to the floor, but she didn't notice. She was too worried about what the intruders would do. The home was well insulated against temperature extremes, but she didn't know if it would stop bullets.

Falyn knew the locked doors wouldn't stop them. All they had to do was break a window to get in. She couldn't let them get that close. She aimed short and squeezed off a shot that exploded in the grass in front of them.

"Stop, right there! The next shot won't miss. Just get back in your flyer and go back wherever you came from."

"Ma'am, we just want to talk," said the one left of center.

"Then talk. I can hear you just fine from there.

"We're from the base. We need you to come there with us."

Falyn squeezed off another shot. This one landed to the left of the group, so close the man on the left end could feel the heat.

"Nice try. I just talked to my mate. He was told that Driscoll sent you. So, he's coming for you."

"I guess we'll do this the hard way." All of them started shooting at the house.

Falyn jumped back from the window and flattened herself on the floor behind the mattress, hoping the added barrier would protect her. She could hear glass breaking, and she could only imagine the mess she would have in the kitchen.

They each must have spent a full magazine shooting up her house. It seemed like it went on far longer than a couple minutes.

"Well, now you've done it!" Muttering, Falyn got to her knees and aimed the rifle out the window. Flipping a switch on the stock, she fired on auto-repeat, sweeping across the four men walking toward her home. They all went down, and none of them got up.

She stared for a moment, checking for movement. She had killed them.

Falyn started to shake as she slid to the floor, holding the ion rifle resting across her lap. She had just killed four men after they tried to kill her. Too stunned to even cry, Falyn just sat there staring straight ahead until she heard the familiar whine of Max's sky cycle.

"Falyn!" Max called frantically. "Falyn, are you alright?"

"Here! I'm up here!" she called out to him, still trembling, unsure whether she could get up or not.

Max bounded up the stairs and stood in front of her in seconds. "Baby, are you alright."

She looked up at him and blinked, trying to find an answer.

Max squatted in front of her searching her face with a concerned expression. "Here, let me have this," he said, slowly reaching for the rifle and gently prying her hands from it. Standing, he flicked on the safety, set the bed upright, and laid the rifle on it.

Chapter Nineteen

Once Max laid the rifle on the bed, he turned back and offered his hands to help Falyn up. Soon as she was on her feet, he pulled her into his arms.

"You're hurt!" he exclaimed at the trickle of blood trailing down from her scalp on the side of her face."

"A splinter from the window frame. I thought they would tear the house down with all their bullets. 'They made a big mistake... Tried to tell me you sent them to take me to the base... I knew better."

"Ah, Falyn Scared me out of my mind when I saw the front of the house. Price was under the impression they wanted to take you alive."

"All that shooting scared the hell out of me."

"They must have given up on taking you alive when you fought back."

Falyn pressed her face against his chest and tightened her arms around him as her trembling gradually subsided.

"I wish I had gotten here faster to protect you."

"No, Max. Don't blame yourself. You gave me the rifle and showed me how to use it. I could never have stopped them with my old pump shotgun," she asserted. "I am glad you are here now."

"I wish I didn't need to go back. I've got two protectors on their way to stand watch here while I handle things in the overlord stronghold."

Falyn nodded against his chest. "I'll be fine."

"They will get the bodies ready to transport and get the flyer out of your field. If anyone else shows up without clearance through me, they will shoot them out of the sky."

Falyn looked up at him with parted lips, raised up on her toes, and pressed them to his. Max caressed her lips with his and deepened the kiss, silently thanking the Universe that he had taught her to use that rifle.

Max seemed as reluctant as she to end the kiss. He didn't want to leave Falyn for a minute, but this was the biggest solo command of his career. His protector teams were well trained before they came to serve with him, but they lacked his combat experience.

Even though they could probably carry out the mission without him, he was responsible for its success or failure. Yet, his mate had been in danger, and he wasn't there. Max knew he would rather face death than lose Falyn.

With his teams wreaking havoc with Thrix's and Driscoll's operation, the probability was low that they would send anyone else after his mate. Knowing that didn't make it any easier to leave her.

"I know you have to go," Falyn said. "This is the world we will raise our children in one day. We don't want human traffickers tied to alien slavers kidnapping people everywhere. You have to stop them."

"I'll be back as soon as possible, my love."

"I'll be here. You said the protectors are very diligent."

Max could tell she was still a little shaky despite what she said. Of course, she was! She had never killed four men before.

"Falyn, you didn't have a choice. With all the damage they caused, they were not caring whether you lived or died. I would have killed them if you hadn't first. They tried to hurt you. That's all I need to know."

Max cradled her face in his hands, looking into her eyes. "You defended yourself. They would have killed you or taken you with them to send off world with an alien slaver. You did nothing wrong. Do you understand?"

Falyn blinked slowly and nodded.

Max kissed her forehead and then her lips softly. As he heard the whine of sky cycles in the distance, he picked up the ion rifle and shouldered it by its strap, then he walked Falyn downstairs.

"Omigod!" shrieked when she saw the damage in the kitchen. "They ruined my kitchen!"

All the windows were broken, and there were bullet holes in every cabinet and wall. Some of the cabinets had glass doors on them, which were all broken, too. It could all be fixed, but it would never be the same again. The cozy kitchen she grew up with was all but destroyed. The house had been in her family for over a hundred years.

Now she was angry. Max suspected she realized that some of those hundreds of bullets were meant for her.

Momentarily, the two sky cycles Max heard stopped midair and slowly descended vertically to the ground. While the two cyborg protectors dismounted, he scanned the barn, the smaller buildings, and the house for intruders, but there were none.

He introduced them to Falyn as Force and Brute. Each bowed his head graciously to Falyn as they were introduced.

"We will protect your female as if she were our own," Brute assured Max while Force bowed his head briefly in agreement.

Max caressed Falyn's cheek with his finger tips and gave her an ardent look before he left to mount his sky cycle. Moments later, he was in the air and off like a shot toward the horizon.

Brute and Force went to move the dead gangers' flyer out of the pasture and load the dead men into it. Meanwhile, Falyn went to the tool shed to get a scoop-shovel to start cleaning the broken glass.

In addition to broken glass, wood splinters were on nearly every surface. She started at the top with the bullet-riddled cupboards. Dishes in her family for over a hundred years were shattered. A few had miraculously survived, but all the heirloom wine glasses in the top of the cupboard were broken.

That's when Falyn started to cry angry tears. Of course, she knew they were all just things. She was alive, and her home could be repaired. None of her animals were harmed, but the broken dishes and wine glasses were all part of her heritage.

Climbing up on a stepstool to survey the damage, she sobbed angrily. These were dishes and glassware her great-great-great grandparents used to serve food and drink. Only a couple of plates remained intact. Hoping at least one of the wine glasses was unbroken, she took one step higher.

Falyn let herself cry for a minute or so after seeing none of the wine glasses intact. "Those bastards!" she cried. They fucking destroyed her kitchen, trying to kill her all because Max was doing his job. Conversely, they never would have come after her if not for Max.

Blaming Max wouldn't be fair. They came to use her against him because they knew how much she meant to him. Losing her would break him. Killing those bastards had saved the life they were making together. They were part of a gang that sold humans to alien slavers who sold them to other aliens to abuse sexually.

When she had cried out her anger and fear, she wiped tears from her eyes with her fingers. She didn't dare to use any cloths in the kitchen because they might hold slivers of glass. She calmed herself with a few deep breaths and picked up the large metal pot and brush from the counter.

Using the long-handled utility brush to keep her hands from getting cut on the glass shards, she swept the remnants of her wine glasses off the shelf and into a large metal pot.

As she moved on to the next shelf, she caught sight of her dining room China cabinet. It was unmarked, and the 'good' dishes had all survived. Her pot filled quickly from one cupboard and the counter beneath.

She carried it outside, trying to decide how to dispose of it. Setting the pot on the porch, she went to the tool shed and got the wheelbarrow leaning against it. She steered it to the porch, parked it, and emptied the pot of broken dishes, glass, and wood splinters into it.

When it was filled, she would start a pile at the edge of the woods surrounding her property and then bury it. That wouldn't be the end of it. Most of the cabinets were damaged beyond repair, but she needed to clear away the broken glass to see if anything was salvageable.

Bullet holes in the cook stove's metal chimney meant it would need to be replaced before she could heat or cook with it. It was midsummer, so heat wouldn't be a problem. There were bullet holes everywhere, worrying Falyn about the structural integrity of the kitchen and porch.

She would clean up first and rescue whatever was salvageable. Max would help her figure it out when his mission was finished.

Chapter Twenty

The raid of the Overlord stronghold was fully underway when Max returned to the urban ruins. Teams of five cyborgs went from structure to structure on four sides of Thrix's territory. Most of them were makeshift dwellings of salvaged materials.

All of the cyborgs were wearing traditional armor except for Max. His armor was integrated within his body and assembled at will by internal nanites. It was impenetrable by bullets from projectile guns, but that didn't stop the gangers from firing non-stop at them as the cyborgs raided them.

Only one member of each team carried an ion rifle because short-range blasters were more effective in close quarters. The protectors either walked right up to the shooters firing at them, ripping their weapons from their hands, or used the blasters to stun them.

Thrix's control center was in the middle of his territory and served as his home. His gangers built theirs surrounding it, so they served as a buffer zone. Unknown to them, he had an underground tunnel that would take him to a hanger outside the buffer to his Mesaarkan escape flyer.

Colton landed his flyer at Thrix's hanger just ahead of the cyborg protectors' landing outside his territory. His com-tablet vibrated in his pocket before he could leave the cockpit.

"Colton, I can't get a hold of Thrix," Driscoll grumbled. "He's not answering his com, and he needs to get out of here before the cyborg teams come. If they find him, they just might kill him."

"Especially those who fought in the war. He's probably in his playroom with one of the females. I'll run over and check."

"Watch yourself," said Driscoll. "He's been known to go ballistic when he's interrupted."

"He doesn't want to test them. They'll waste him in a heartbeat if they find him balls deep in a human female."

"That will be his problem," said Colton as he started jogging through the tunnel to Thrix's lair.

Colton heard the cries and moans of a female as he entered Thrix's dwelling. Just as they thought, the Mesaarkan was tormenting some female. Then he heard the female wailing in pain. As he listened, he heard a slapping sound before the next scream.

At that point, the female started to sob as Colton moved stealthily down the narrow hallway to the Mesaarkan's sadistic playroom. The door was open wide enough for Colton to see inside. The Mesaarkan had some blond female strapped spreadeagle and face down on a horizontal X-cross on a swivel, fucking her.

Colton thought the Mesaarkan was probably the only one enjoying it as she wept softly. The reptilian lashed her with the whip-like end of his tail, eliciting another painful scream from her.

The cyborg convert hated himself for helping to provide human females for Mesaarkans like Thrix to abuse.

"Hey, Thrix. Hurry up and shoot your wad; we need to get out of here," Colton called after he had backed down the hall a dozen feet.

"Colt?"

Price stopped as he heard the voice; he'd begun to believe he would never hear again. "Tessa?"

"Colt!" she sobbed.

The cyborg strode to the wooden door and flung it open with such force that the top hinge pulled apart. "You fucking lizard, get off of her!"

Colton grabbed his tail and yanked the Mesaarkan back. "You bastard! You've had her all this time, and you knew she is mine." He grabbed the alien's arm and jerked him around so he could smash a fist into Thrix's face.

The Mesaarkan flew out of the room and into the hallway's far wall. Colton followed, pounding the male's torso while dodging blows from the alien. Mesaarkans weren't as strong and fast as even converted cyborgs. Colt pressed his advantage, kicking and punching Thrix without mercy.

"Fuck! Price, she is just a female. We have dozens. Take one of them."

"You asshole! They are not interchangeable. Tessa's been mine since we were kids. After I showed you her hologram, you knew this female you called Connie was my Contessa. You kept her hidden every time I came to see if she came in with a new batch. All this time, you've been fucking torturing her."

Thrix was not helpless and got in blows of his own, knocking Colton on his ass and bloodying his nose. Thrix tried to kick the cyborg in the crotch, but Colton blocked and shoved him back, pushing himself back onto his feet. The alien's face was swelling, and one of his eyes was puffed closed.

"I've had enough, Price. I'm leaving. Take the female; I don't care," said Thrix starting to walk away."

Colton turned to the horizontal cross Tessa was strapped, pulling out his combat knife to cut her loose. A sound behind him stopped him.

"Pivoting, Colton plunged the long, sharp blade into Thrix. The Mesaarkan grunted in pain while Colton pulled it out and stabbed him again.

Both wounds would kill him without medical intervention, but Colton wasn't finished. Thrix staggered, turning to face him, and Colton shoved him into the wall pressing his forearm against the alien's throat. Holding him there as blood loss made Thrix too weak to fight back, Colton stabbed the knife into the alien's abdomen several more times, once in the groin.

The alien had his wife the whole time, torturing her and fucking her while Colton was going out of his mind from his loss.

The reptilian gagged and grunted with each puncture. "It didn't have to come to this, Thrix. You could have just given her back to me when you knew." By then, Thrix had stopped fighting. Colton was the only reason he hadn't sunk to the floor. He was clearly dying, so Colton backed away, letting him slide to the floor. "Why didn't you?

"Because I love her…." Then he died.

"You don't know the meaning of the word, you arrogant prick." Colton kicked him in the head then wiped the blood off his knife across Thrix's chest and sheathed it.

Finally, he turned and went into the sadistic 'playroom. Tessa was crying, and no wonder. Her back was striped with red welts, and a few were bleeding. Her butt cheeks were pinkened with Mesaarkan hand prints and scratches from his claws.

"Don't cry, baby. I'm going to get you out of here and take you home," he soothed.

Colton needed to get her out of there before the Enclave cyborgs came. Colton didn't doubt that by now they knew he'd been working for Thrix, but he hinted to Max that he was still a Federation agent even if he had gone a little rogue on the operation.

Ripping off the straps that held her arms and legs, he tried to lift her off the contraption without increasing her pain.

That was nearly impossible. When he turned her over, he discovered her nipples painfully crushed in some large clamps. Tessa cried out as he carefully removed them and scooped her up in his arms.

"It's going to be all right, Tessa. I've got you now," Colton murmured and kissed her forehead tenderly.

"Oh, Colt, I missed you so much!" she cried and put her arms around his neck.

"Me, too, baby."

Scanning the room, he found no clothing or blankets to wrap her.

Carrying her down the hall, he discovered a closet holding bedsheets and towels. He pulled out a sheet and stood Tessa on her feet to wrap her in it. He would worry about clothing after he got her someplace safe. Once she was covered, Colton lifted her in his arms, hurrying toward the front door.

Before he reached it, it burst open, letting in a team of six Enclave cyborgs. One of them receded his helmet, revealing Max Steele.

Colton's heart sank. He hadn't just bent a few rules; he'd gone completely rogue and broken laws. "Look, I'm not one of them. Everything I did was to find my wife. And I finally found her. I want to take her home, and you'll never have to see me again."

"You almost killed Stalker," Max accused.

"Only because I thought he was going to kill me. I went there to get back the Mesaarkan flyer for Thrix to keep on his good side until I found Tessa. But, he's dead, so it doesn't matter now," Colton explained. "Come on, Max! What would you do if someone sold your mate to the Mesaarkans?"

"I would end them," Max replied without hesitation.

"So, you understand. Please, let us leave, and I swear you will never see or hear about me again. I have a place in the mountains back east. I just want to go home and live with Tessa in peace."

Max looked at Colton, then at the woman, he held, clinging to him, wrapped in a sheet. There was a bruise on her face and bruises on her arms. Finally, the cyborg ranger nodded and stepped aside. The other cyborgs moved out of the way so he could pass.

Once Colton left, Max and his team searched the house. They only found a dead Mesaarkan propped against the wall in front of the doorway into the BDSM chamber of horror. That in itself was not shocking. But considering a Mesaarkan was using it, those activities weren't consensual.

Technically, Colton could be sent to the prison planet. But he'd fought in the same war the rangers fought. He'd lost a part of his humanity and returned to find his wife stolen.

Max knew that if someone stole Falyn, he would go on a tear and beat down anyone who got in his way. He had a pretty good idea of what Tessa had been through. She'd hung on for Colton to find her. Whatever Colton might deserve for his methods, she didn't. Max's decision was for her, not Colton.

Chapter Twenty-One

The gangers on guard at Thrix's residence had tried to flee when they saw Max's team approach. They didn't get far before the cyborgs dropped all four of them with stun blasts. Inside the building, the guard at the harem's suite dropped his weapon and surrendered.

The women were frightened when Max entered in his shiny dark gray armor. Retracting his helmet helped because the young, handsome cyborg didn't look at them with lust in his eyes even though most were scantily clad.

"Females, please remain calm. I am Lieutenant Max Steel of the Cyborg Rangers. We are here to free you. All the buildings and wreckage in this part of the city will be leveled and cleared away starting two days from now, and we are evacuating everyone."

"But where will we go?" a young woman asked.

"East to our base, where we will provide you with food and shelter while demolition and new home construction proceeds. The Enclave has provided medics and educators to help you transition into modern living and homesteading trades. Gather your belongings and be ready for transport in fifteen minutes."

A few other women called out questions. While he knew most of the answers, he needed to interrogate Driscoll. "The Enclave liaisons will answer your questions when you get to the shelter. I have other duties right now."

As Max made his way through the cluttered streets toward Driscoll's residence, he was glad he used a minimum violence plan. He hadn't realized how many females and children lived among the ruins. Most of them were gangers' families. Working for the overlord was how they provided for their mates and children.

He hoped their loyalties were stronger for their families than the overlords. Neither Max nor the Enclave wanted to separate fathers from their families. They would be given a choice to abide by Enclave laws and remain with their families or go offworld to Penta Prison Planet.

He wouldn't be offering that deal to Driscoll. He was second in command to Ven'Rel Thrix in trafficking humans to the Mesaarkans, who had nearly destroyed Earth.

When Max arrived, Driscoll was seated in a plastic chair with his hands zip-tied behind his back and his ankles tied to the front chair legs. He eyed Max warily when he came into the tiny room.

"I've got two choices for you, Driscoll. I doubt you want either one of them, but one is better than the other."

"What choices? Whether you kill me slowly and painful or fast and painless?" the prisoner sneered.

"Mr. Driscoll, it's not up to me to determine your punishment; that's for the court to decide. Because you were trafficking humans to alien slavers, odds are good you will be shipped to Penta Prison Planet.

"Whether you cooperate or not will make a difference which Colony you'll live in—the primitive barbaric underground mining colony, or the secure settlement with amenities such as food and shelter and low competition for necessities."

Max used his com-tablet to present holograms of each part of the penal colony as he spoke. He showed the mine with prisoners working under horrific conditions along with prisoners fighting to the death for whatever reason.

Driscoll cringed visibly and closed his eyes.

Max shut that one off and waited before he showed the second choice. He could live in the farming colony and work a few hours a day growing and processing food for the rest of the settlement. There he would have a private residence with overseers that kept order among the inmates and no separations of the sexes.

The threat of transfer to the mines incentivized them to behave and follow the rules.

"It's your choice," Max said finally.

"What do I have to do?"

"Give us Gergis."

"How the hell am I going to do that?"

"When and where is he going to land?"

"He doesn't land his ship. He sends a shuttle from orbit to here and one to the starport. The shuttle for here is cloaked. By this last communication, he should come sometime next week."

"Are you his main contact, or was it Thrix?" Max asked.

"I am," Driscoll admitted reluctantly.

"We want you to get him to send the shuttle for your captives and give us the landing coordinates. We'll do the rest," said Max.

"And I don't go to the mines?"

"I will make that request."

"Request? That's not good enough. I need a guarantee, or you get nothing."

"In that case, you are guaranteed to go to the mines. If I make the request, the odds are 91.6% they will act on my recommendation, especially if it gives them Gergis."

"Fuck!" Driscoll grumbled. "Alright, I'll do it."

"Good choice." Momentarily, two cyborgs entered the tiny room. "These protectors will take you back to our base to

201

secure lockup, where you will receive basic necessities. We have your com-tablet and will monitor it until you're needed to communicate with Gergis."

Max turned abruptly and left as the protectors freed Driscoll's legs and escorted him to the transport. Everything was under control, so he was going home to Falyn.

His plan was simple. When the slaver's shuttle landed to pick up the victims, the cyborgs would take control and return the shuttle to the slaver's ship filled with cyborgs. The cyborgs would seize the vessel, arrest the crew and rescue any captives.

Max would lead that team because bringing down the human traffickers would bring order to all their territories. That would make it safer for people to settle in and build families. But foremost in his mind was keeping Falyn safe.

In a civilized society, he should be able to leave his home without worrying whether his mate would be safe alone. Max was still angry that she had been terrorized by those thugs. Granted, they paid with their lives, but they didn't experience the fear Falyn faced before they died.

Then his thoughts drifted back to Colton Price finally finding his wife. How would she get over the horror of her captivity? He hoped Colton would be astute enough to get help for her.

Would Falyn need therapy to deal with her ordeal?

He wished the sky cycle would go faster so he could be with her sooner. Only, he was already flying at top speed, and every minute still felt like ten. Max stopped at the base mess hall to make things easier by picking up dinner for them.

He thanked Force and Brute for securing the homestead while he was gone and dismissed them. They had come on one sky cycle to take the flyer and the bodies back to the base for processing.

Max was surprised when he arrived to find the front door reattached with its window boarded over and the kitchen cleaned. His men indicated that Falyn was in the barn, so he set the self-heating container on the counter by the sink and went back out to find her.

Falyn had just finished milking and set the last goat off the milking stand. She looked up and smiled as she heard Max enter. He deliberately scuffed his foot on the floor so she wouldn't be startled.

They came together in a heartfelt hug and a smoldering kiss. "I am so sorry that happened to you," Max murmured. "I was missing factors when I calculated the possibility that the enemy would come after you. We had a spy posing as a refugee." He gazed down at her, continuing to hold her in his arms.

"I am much better now that you're here. I am spitting mad about what they did to my kitchen."

"I'll get someone here to fix it as it was with any improvements you'd like. I have pictures in my CPU of the room before the damage."

"I am glad you weren't damaged during your mission if you had to face men with weapons like those."

"We had armor to protect us. Our only concern was that they might have some Mesaarkan high-tech weapons. They didn't."

"So, what happened to them?"

"We stun blasted them and took them all alive. The only casualty was the Mesaarkan, Thrix. Colton Price killed him after catching him apparently raping his wife."

"How awful for her!"

"I should have arrested him for going completely rogue. He almost killed Neely and Stalker, plus he did kill an eastern overlord."

"But you didn't. How come?"

"His wife needed him. She didn't deserve to be punished for what he did. I told Stalker, but he agreed the female needed Colton more than Stalker needed revenge." Max explained.

"I think that was a good decision," Falyn agreed. "I'm done out here, now. Let's get the milk in the pasteurizer and go into the house."

"We can have dinner, and you can welcome me home," he said with a sexy smirk, nuzzling her neck.

"I knew you'd see it my way." She giggled. "But I don't know what we're going to eat. I couldn't fire up the stove with holes in the pipe.

"Exactly why I brought dinner from the mess hall. It will stay warm until we're ready to   eat."

Chapter Twenty-Two

Max initiated another smoldering kiss once the milk was set to pasteurize. He ended it, carrying Falyn into the house with her wrapped around him. By then, the scent of her arousal had made him hard as a rock.

Getting her naked was even quicker than usual because she wore a standard issue khaki t-shirt and black cargo pants instead of handmade. The handmade cotton pants and tunics had ties and buttons, and haste could pop buttons off and rip seams.

Max shed his clothes in seconds, then went to work on Falyn's. Pushing her cargo pants to the floor, he knelt in front of her after she toed off her new boots. That made him the perfect height to take one of her taut nipples into his mouth and suckle it while kneading her other breast and plucking that nipple with his fingers.

Falyn moaned, cradling his head and running her fingers through his short-cropped hair. As he moved to suck on her other nipple, he slid his hand between her leg, brushing her clit before he pushed a finger deep into her opening.

"Aah," she moaned, holding his head to her breast. She murmured his name, and her knees nearly buckled when he pressed his thumb against her clit.

Max stopped what he was doing, scooping her up as he stood and laid her on the bed, climbing on with her. Laying over her, with a thick, muscular thigh between her legs, he nuzzled her neck, then drew his lips along her jawline and to her lips.

He slipped his tongue into her mouth as his lips settled over hers. She swirled her tongue around his in a sensual dance and stroked his back lovingly.

Max wanted everything from her, to kiss and caress her, to feast on her cream and fuck her long and hard until she screamed his name as she climaxed.

Falyn could feel his erection against her thigh as he moved between her legs. Her body throbbed with desire, and she would have been happy to take his cock then. Only it quickly became clear that Max was taking the full tour.

He worked his way down her body, paying homage to her breasts, kneading them with his hands and sucking each nipple until she squirmed beneath him.

"Oh, Max," she crooned. "You make me feel so good." He could make her forget her own name and the four thugs who terrorized her that day.

She murmured words of encouragement and made soft sounds of pleasure, caressing his head and shoulders as he moved lower on her belly. Then she felt his breath on her mons as he parted the dark curls, and she started to pant.

Drawing her knees up, Falyn spread her legs wide, giving Max full access. He drew his tongue up through her slit, lapping at her juices and eliciting heartfelt moans from her.

A wave of excruciating pleasure caused her to cry out when his lips settled over her sensitive clit. Max curled his arms around her thighs to hold her still while he worked his magic. Alternately licking and gently sucking, he was driving her mad with such intense pleasure to the verge of orgasm. Then he stopped.

"Omigod! Max, don't stop," she cried, ending with a whimper.

"Do you love me?"

"Oh, God, yes. Of course, I love you!"

"Will you marry me?"

"Huh? Aren't we already?"

"I mean the way people used to with family and friends."

"Ah, Max! Whatever you want! Please, I need to come.... I need. Argh!"

With her assent, he went back to flicking his tongue over her clit and alternately sucking it.

"Max!" Falyn screamed a second later as the first wave of a powerful orgasm racked her body. It hit her so hard that Max was somewhat challenged to hold her in place.

She sobbed and shrieked, pushing his head as she became too sensitive. Even after he pulled back, her hips bucked with the hard orgasmic contractions of her womb. Aftershocks rippled through her body even after Max lay beside her, taking her into his arms.

Falyn put her arms around him and pressed her breasts against his chest. His hard length lay between her legs, pressing against her core.

Still shaking intermittently, Falyn rubbed his back and caressed his head as she kissed his neck, murmuring his name and telling him how much she loved him.

"Falyn, sweetheart, I love you so much; those words barely touch my feelings. That you love me back is more than I dared to hope. You are my heart, and I will protect you with my life."

They kissed and cuddled for a few more minutes before Max rolled her beneath him. "Are you ready for this?" He dragged the length of his cock up over her mons and poised its head at her opening.

"Oh, yeah!" Her eyes widened, and she groaned as his cock filled her wet heat.

"Look at me while I breed with you." It was worded as a command but spoken as a request.

Falyn smiled at him and gripped his shoulders as he began pumping in and out of her. Watching his face as he fucked her, she knew without a doubt this cyborg owned her heart as he staked his claim repeatedly with every thrust of his cock.

He slammed into her again and again, hitting her G-spot and rubbing her clit almost every time. Quivers of delight rippled through her, steadily raising her toward a pinnacle of ecstasy she had never reached before.

She continued holding his gaze even as he pounded into her, only closing her eyes briefly each time she came. What an incredible turn-on! She could see her future in his eyes, dark and intense with desire born of love. Falyn lost track of how many orgasms she had, or maybe it was one long one that ebbed and flowed until Max pumped his nanite-laden semen into her womb with a roar.

Watching him, Falyn thought he was nothing short of magnificent. *Mine!*

"Mine!" Max repeated almost as though he'd read her thoughts. Then he kissed her tenderly.

Every battle on every planet they dropped his team, fighting day after day, year after year, brought him to this moment. Falyn was the mate he'd waited for all his life, and now she was his for the rest of it. He could only smile as he lifted his lips from hers and rubbed his nose back and forth over hers.

Colton Price carried his wife, Tessa, to his flyer near where Thrix kept his. He considered stealing Thrix's superior model, but he didn't want to give Max any reason to change his mind. Tessa whimpered when he set her in the passenger seat of his flyer.

He wasn't surprised after seeing the welts on her back and dark pink hand prints on her buttocks. Swearing under his breath, he wished he could kill Thrix again and make him suffer more for what he had done to Tessa. The filthy lizard was a sadist in his sexual pursuits. It was sexual torture.

After a session in Thrix's playroom, a female would take days to recover without medical intervention. That's why he needed a harem.

Colton went to the storage compartment behind the seats and took out a bolus of universal nanites from his med kit. "Baby, I need to squirt this up your nose. It's going to make you feel better."

"Is it *seronome*?" Tessa sounded hopeful.

"No, sweetie, just nanites to heal your injuries."

Tessa sighed. "Okay. Thrix always gave me *seronome* before and after I submit. It makes me forget the pain."

So, he hooked her on a Mesaarkan euphoria drug on top of everything he had done to her. There was no way he could just take her home and pretend it never happened.

He would have to take her to Starport City Medical Clinic in Farringay. Tessa needed neuro-psychotherapy and detox before he could expect to share a normal life with her.

Stowing the syringe, he closed the passenger door and walked around to the flyer. Dropping into the pilot's seat, he closed the door. Squeezing his eyes shut, he grimaced. How could he ever unsee Thrix fucking his wife strapped into that evil contraption? Maybe he needed a little neuro-psychotherapy himself.

Maybe then the nightmare would really be over.

Chapter Twenty-Three

A week and a half later, Gergis arrived in orbit and sent two shuttles to land on Earth. One with legitimate cargo went to the starport in Farringay, and the other landed at a former park near the building where potential slaves were being held. Only those abductees were at Max's base of operations preparing for planned new lives in the town.

Driscoll had fulfilled their agreement and called the shuttle down to the usual landing spot. He was terrified of the underground prison-run mines on Penta. He was not the tough guy he pretended to be for the gangers. His hand-to-hand fighting skills were strictly mediocre. But he could shoot, and he could run. Neither would help him escape from the cyborgs. So, he cooperated.

Max and a team of ten armed cyborg protectors were waiting to board the slave shuttle when it landed. Soon as the loading ramp was extended, he scanned it through his internal CPU to locate all the beings aboard it. He discovered eight other beings besides the pilot and copilot. His team had discerned the same intel, so Max gave them their tasks for the raid through the cyborg network.

Armed and armored, Max led the team into the huge freight shuttle. The Mesaarkan medic at the first station was shocked and horrified to greet an armored cyborg with a blaster pointed at his face. He put up his hands in surrender, not daring to move. His job was to scan the abductees for health problems and inject them with microchips to track them.

The other personnel were strategically placed to force the captives into various holding cells. They were armed only with shock sticks which didn't work on armored cyborgs. Most of them were not human but various species from the Mesaarkan Conglomerate worlds.

These alien humanoids knew they were no match for armed cyborgs, plus they knew their rights. The Federation-Mesaarkan peace agreement specified that citizens of the Conglomerate who broke Federation law could only be deported back to the Conglomerate. They chose to save themselves by surrendering.

No one on Max's team was surprised. They quickly secured all of the aliens into the cells meant for the human slaves. Next, they went after the pilots, who were unarmed and human. Max convinced them they would be killed if they didn't fly the shuttle back up to the main ship.

However, to avoid suspicion, they had to wait two hours to launch because it would have taken that long to process seventy slaves for transport. Max used that time to interrogate them about the freighter's layout, defenses, and personnel. They already had a hundred humans abducted from backwater colonies, plus various humanoids from planets allied with the Federation.

Seizing the slave ship was almost anticlimactic after all of fighting with the overlords and gangers in the cyborgs' quest to end human trafficking in the ruined metropolitan areas around North America. The abductions were not, however, limited to North America. Three ships were picking up abductees all over the world. They had only made the initial breakthrough in North America with the cyborg rangers.

They had not been caught because the slave ships had new Mesaarkan cloaking technology unavailable during the war. To further avoid detection, they would come to Earth by approaching orbit keeping Earth between their ship and the Federation *Starfire Nemesis*.

None of Gergis's crew were willing to fight the armed and armored cyborgs, not even Gergis. The crew was put into the slaves' cells, and the prospective slaves were freed and taken to Max's base of operations. The former prison was big enough to house thousands more than were currently housed there.

Capturing the slave ship was quite a prestigious accomplishment for the cyborg ranger. Before finding Falyn, Max would have been thrilled with his team's achievement. Now, he was relieved that he could retire from the rangers, go back to the mountains, and continue building a life with Falyn.

Max thought it ironic that he'd never wanted the post in Northern California. He had only accepted it to fulfill his duty as a cyborg ranger. What he'd initially thought was a sacrifice brought him to the life he had only dreamed of.

Star Force pilots arrived to take over the slave ship and shuttles a few hours after Max's team seized the ship. They transported the cyborgs and the captives back to Earth in shuttles. Having been alerted to the situation, the Enclave sent aid workers to Max's base to sort out the rescues and arrange for them to return to their home planets if they so desired. Those who wanted to remain on Earth would be assimilated into the various communities.

As soon as that was organized, Max was heading back to Falyn in the mountains on his sky cycle. He resigned before he left Rexas Strong in charge, recommending that the former newbie cyborg be put in charge of the northern California territory.

Rexas had only been awakened for about five years. Unlike Max, he didn't have almost a brutal hundred years of war experience behind him. (91.72 years to be exact.) He wanted the life he was promised for putting in those years of combat. His team stopped the human trafficking by the slavers. Star Force could track down the rest.

It had been three days since he'd seen Falyn other than on his com-tablet.

She must have been listening for him because she was waiting for him on the back porch. Wearing nothing but that flimsy little robe that gaped open the front with nothing under it, she ran down the steps and jumped into his arms.

Falyn pressed her lips to his without a word, but no words were necessary. Her hair was damp, and she smelled like lavender mingled with the scent of her arousal. Max mounted the steps, still kissing her. He pressed her against the wall beside the kitchen door and opened the closure on his pants with its usual ripping sound.

"Is this what you want?" he whispered close to her lips."

"Yes, my love," she whispered back.

She groaned in satisfied bliss as he slid his cock into her wet tunnel.

Falyn murmured a series of pleasure sounds as he started thrusting hard and deep, pausing to rub his flesh against her clit. He gradually moved a little faster, bringing her to her first climax and nursing her through it to draw out her enjoyment.

"Ah, Max. I'm so glad your home."

"Me, too, Baby. Are you ready to go again?" he asked, still inside her.

"Oh, yeah!"

For whatever reason, it turned her on when he took her on the back porch in front of nature. Max was more than happy to oblige.

Later, when she finished welcoming him home, he would tell her the news.

Chapter Twenty-Four

Colton Price blinked his eyes open, startled at the unfamiliar surroundings, until he remembered where he was. He was in a medical bed, awakening from neuro-psychotherapy. He'd decided he needed it as much as Tessa after the nightmare his last two years had been, that simply compounded his time in the war and being transformed into a cyborg.

They used a combination of nanotechnology and biologics to dull memories that elicited a painful emotional response. There was always the risk other memories could be damaged or erased. All he cared about was that he would remember Tessa and love her. Nothing else mattered to him.

A medic wearing a badge that said 'Dr. Rand Jeffreys' came into the treatment room as he slowly sat on the bed. He confirmed that Colton remembered who he was and why he was there.

"Now, can I see Tessa?"

"Yes, she just woke up and is asking for you," the young male medic said. "Go ahead and get dressed, and I will come to get you."

Colton pulled on the standard issue in less than a minute. He was about to go looking for the medic when his com beeped. Pulling it from his pocket, he looked at the message. It was from Eddie: "Took your advice. I met a girl at the camp. We're getting a homestead. Now I understand about Tessa. Glad you found her. I'll be in touch."

Colton smiled as he closed the com. The kid was going to be okay.

Finally, he went out in the hall, looking for the medic.

He was nowhere in sight, but he heard Tessa's voice coming from a room two doors down. He walked to the room and stopped beside the door; worried Tessa might not want him as a cyborg.

What if everything had changed after the hell she'd been through and the tricky neuro-psychotherapy she'd received?

"Of course, I want to see him!" Tessa asserted to the medic. "Does he not want to see me?"

"No, he wants to see you. I was just making sure you are up to it."

"Well, why do you think I asked? He's my husband. It's been five years."

Colton took that as his cue to enter the room. "Well, I am here now. How do you feel?"

"Like I've just awakened from a horrible nightmare that I can't quite remember."

"Don't even try, honey." He went to her, where she was sitting on the edge of the bed, and hugged her.

Putting her arms around him, hugging him back, she said, "Colt, I missed you so much."

"No more than I missed you, Tessa." He cradled her face in his hands and kissed her tenderly. "Remember that cabin in the mountains we talked about in our vid exchanges?"

"It's ready and waiting for us."

"Oh, but our flat needs to be packed up and cleared."

"Done."

"But, how? You just got back." Tessa frowned, searching his face, trying to understand.

Colton looked to the medic, uncertain how or if he should tell her about the time loss.

"Mrs. Price, the nightmare you can't remember wasn't just a nightmare. You lived it. We don't even know everything that happened to you. It's been two years since your husband returned from the war to find you missing. When you didn't return, your belongings were packed and put into storage, so you no longer have a flat." Dr. Jeffreys explained.

"Two years? What was I doing for two years? I was getting ready to meet Colt's shuttle at the star port yesterday."

"Tessa, trust me, you don't want to know. I still remember the facts, but not like I lived it. None of it was your fault. People hurt you, and I don't want you to remember how bad it was."

She studied his face for a moment. "By the look in your eyes, it must have been bad."

"Give it some time, Mrs. Price. Learning the facts at this point could trigger those painful memories. The longer it takes for them to surface, the less likely you will be severely affected."

"Telling me I don't want to know makes me more curious than ever. On the other hand, whatever kept me away from Colt for two years when I'd been counting the days until he would come home must be pretty scary." She sighed. "And, I don't feel like two years are missing from my life, I'm guessing, thanks to your treatment. I woke up happy despite the vague remnants of a nightmare because today is Colt's homecoming."

"In a way, it is. Are you ready to go see our cabin?"

"What about my stuff?"

"It'll be drone dropped in a couple days."

"But I have nothing but this to wear."

"Do you really think you'll need to worry about something to wear?" He gave her a suggestive smirk that made her blush. "Anyway, I have a cleaner."

"You two are all set," said Dr. Jeffreys. "You can be on your way."

A half-hour later, Colton set down the flyer beside his small Blue Ridge cabin in a meadow just a half mile east of Enclave territory. He'd picked that spot because there were no roads through the thick forest that covered most of it. That made it unlikely anyone would inadvertently wander onto the property.

"It's adorable," Tessa said as they landed in front of it.

"It's only three rooms and a bathroom, but we can get additions as we need them."

"For our kids? You still want them?"

"Only if you want them too."

"I do, but not right away. I missed you so much while you were gone; I want time for just us."

"I'd like that, too." Colton smiled at her and opened the flyer's doors. He climbed out and went around to help Tessa unharness. Taking her hand as she stepped out, he led her to the cabin.

The door slid open automatically when Colton stepped in front of it. They entered the kitchen/dining area. There was a traditional cooker and a food processor in the kitchen and a square table with four chairs in the dining area. The living room was perpendicular to the dining area with the entrance to the bedroom off the living room.

"This is everything we talked about," Tessa beamed as they stopped in front of the bedroom door.

"Say 'open,'" Colt told her.

Tessa did, and the door slid open. The room was dark blue with a huge bed in the middle. Across from the entrance, the en suite was opened. Inside, she could see a deep tub big enough for two people. It also contained a shower, sink, and toilet, but only the tub was visible through the open doorway.

As they stepped inside, Tessa glanced at the bathroom tub and then turned her attention to the huge bed in front of her, made up with a contrasting blue cover and two large pillows.

Colton wanted her badly but didn't want to rush her because of her ordeal and their seven years apart. He feared triggering those memories if she felt pressured.

Tessa turned to him, stepping close until her breasts pressed against his lower chest.

She slid her hands up over his chest and clasped them behind his neck, leaning into him as she always had when she wanted sex. He was almost afraid to put his arms around her.

"Do you think we should christen this bed?" she pressed her belly against his erection, making it clear what she meant without words.

"Do you want to?" He looked down at her hopefully.

With an affectionate smile, she nodded.

Colton groaned and bowed his head to claim her lips in a long, slow kiss.

It was so good to be home. Colton didn't care if they never left again as long as Tessa was there with him.

Chapter Twenty-Five

It was almost a mating frenzy from when Max returned to the homestead to evening chores. The last time was in their bed. Falyn lay on her back, naked and blissfully exhausted.

Max lay on his side with his head propped on one hand while he stroked Falyn over her torso. He casually massaged her breasts and teased her nipples into stiff peaks.

It felt so good; she didn't want to stop him even though she felt aroused again. But she could hardly move a muscle, let alone embark on another round of sex. She was not a cyborg after all.

"When is your next mission?" she asked to distract from the throbbing of her clit.

"I've given my resignation."

"What?" her eyes widened as she turned to meet his gaze. "Why would you do that? Don't get me wrong. If it means you'll be around more, I am thrilled."

"Even though it's been a few years, going to war day after day for a future I might never see—I've had enough. Now that I have you, I want to spend my time with you. I want to help you run the homestead and get that horse we talked about."

"That sounds wonderful," she murmured on a sigh followed by a gasp as Max's finger glided over her clit.

"And we have a wedding to plan," he added, sliding two fingers inside her with his thumb working her sensitive bud.

"Max… Oh, Oohh!" Her hips bucked as a full-blown orgasm shook her. She looked up at Max, who was looking quite satisfied with himself. He leaned down to kiss her as his intimate caresses kept her release going.

His kiss was deep and intimate, leaving her wanting more when he lifted his lips from hers. "I couldn't leave you hanging like that." He gave her his classic sexy smile, and Falyn giggled.

"You rest. I'll take care of chores and make dinner."

"I love you."

"And I love you." He gave her a light kiss on the lips. "By the way, we located the gangers' families, and they want the horses."

"Of course, they do. They are all nice horses. I will miss them."

"The Enclave is setting up a secure community for the gangers and their families instead of sending them to prison. If they prove themselves, they will eventually get homesteads outside supervision."

Max rolled off the bed and started pulling on his clothes. "We will get some more horses. I have made inquiries for a draft horse." As he finished dressing, he added, "get some rest."

Pulling up the covers from the bottom of the bed over her. He bent to kiss her cheek, and then he was gone.

Max had a smile on his face the whole time he did the chores. The dream he'd fought his entire life for was finally coming to fruition. Falyn had changed his life in so many ways.

Breeding with her was exquisite, and she was an enthusiastic partner. As the nanites he shared with her built up and multiplied inside, she became less tired after lengthy breeding sessions. After they'd had time to grow in their relationship, they would start their family in a couple of years.

For now, he just wanted her all to himself. Once they had children to care for, there would be no more spontaneous breeding on the porch, kitchen table, or even in the barn. Maybe by then, he would be ready to share her with offspring.

Leaving the chicken coop with the full basket of eggs two hours later, he found Falyn on the kitchen porch, leaning beside the door. Her sexy little robe was tied loosely at the waist and opened in a wide vee, revealing the inner sides of her breasts and just a hint of the dark hair between her legs.

She never looked more beautiful. Max went hard as soon as he saw her. He wasn't sure if she would be there or not; she had been so sleepy when he left her.

Falyn gave him a little smile, watching him approach. She kept her hands behind her back, arching it to make her breasts more prominent. Max never took his eyes off her as he mounted the four steps. Setting the eggs on the little table, he approached and stood in front of her. Holding her gaze, he untied the robe's belt, pushing apart the sides, so the whole front of her body was bared for him.

Max looked down at her breasts and cupped them in his hands, flicking his thumbs over them. Falyn sucked in a breath, drawing his attention back to her eyes. Then he pinched them hard enough to get her full attention. The scent of her arousal grew stronger.

He was about to lift her against the wall as was their normal ritual, but Falyn gripped the waist of his pants and pulled open the closure. She pushed his pants down, kneeling in front of him, his hard cock practically in her face.

She took it in her hands and stroked its silky length. Holding the tip near her mouth, she licked off a drop of precum from the end. She used her lips and tongue up and down his length, then took the head into her mouth. Swirling her tongue around the head, she began sucking on it and bobbing her head back and forth, working the rest with her hands.

Watching, he braced himself with his hands against the wall. Max stifled the urge to thrust into her mouth, but he didn't want to gag her. What a surprising turn on to watch her on her knees sucking his cock. He was surprised because he only expected to give her a quick, hard fuck.

As he felt his release tightening in his lower back, Max decided to let her take it as far as she wanted instead of stopping her. He groaned as the first stream shot down her throat.

She swallowed as fast as possible, making a valiant effort to gulp it all. But she choked as it came too quickly and pulled back, letting his cock slip out of her mouth. Semen ran down her chin and dripped onto her chest. The rest squirted over her breasts, some running down and dripping off the taut peaks of her nipples.

Falyn looked up at him sheepishly and shrugged.

Max grinned down at her. "Baby, that was awesome." He held out his hands and helped her up. "I think I need to take you in the shower."

Pulling up his pants, he put his cock inside and closed the fly. Grabbed the basket of eggs and took her hand, leading her into the house.

"I'll do better next time," she said.

"That was perfect." He set the eggs on the counter by the sink on the way to the bathroom.

Falyn turned on the shower and pushed the robe off her shoulders, letting it drop to the floor, stepping into the water spray. Max pulled his shirt over his head in time to see her rubbing her hands over her breasts, washing off the cum. Seeing her do that hardened his cock all over again.

Toeing the auto release on his boots, he shoved down his pants and stepped out of them. He walked into the water spray in front of her, letting it rinse him off before he turned off the water. Lifting her in his arms, he kissed her deeply, his tongue probing and caressing inside her mouth. She wrapped her arms around his shoulders and her legs around his waist, rubbing her sensitive breasts against his muscular chest.

Without breaking the kiss, he cupped her buttocks in his hands and aligned his cock with her opening. Sliding in to the hilt, he pressed her against the smooth wall. Falyn moaned, clinging to him as he drove his length into her.

"Oh, Max….! So good…" she encouraged him.

He held her, so his arms cushioned her body from the hard wall as he pounded his cock into her.

"Max, Omigod Max, don't stop," she sobbed. After that, she could only moan and croon her pleasure until the intensity of her orgasm made her scream his name, followed by a series of inarticulate wails.

That quickly sent Max over the summit, and he shouted his ecstasy as her inner walls squeezed his cock with the force of her orgasmic contractions, milking his semen until they were both spent.

"Ah, my Falyn. My beautiful mate being with you like this fills me with joy, and I love you more than I ever dreamed." He said the words, looking straight into her eyes, so she knew he meant them.

"Before you came into my life, I was merely surviving. You were what was missing. And I love you with all my heart."

Chapter Twenty-Six

Two Months Later

All the members of Max's ranger team had converged on Falyn's and now his homestead with their mates two days before their wedding. Vyken Dark and his wife Danya also came to lead the ceremony.

Since the bombing of Earth, marriage had become a registration process, and ceremonies were optional. Max had seen one in the entertainment archives and hadn't thought about it again until he claimed Falyn as his mate.

When Max sent out the invitation to his brothers in arms, they didn't just want to attend; they wanted to be part of the ceremony and marry their mates, too. Vyken was invited because he had called them back to Earth, leading them to find their genetic mates.

Six portable prefab huts stood in a row at the meadow's edge at the tree line to house each couple separately. Everyone had gotten new clothing for the wedding. The cyborgs wore military dress uniforms and gathered near the rough-hewn trellis archway, swapping stories of evacuating the ruins for rebuilding each of their territories. They had been dressed and groomed for an hour before the appointed time.

Their mates were getting ready in the house. Falyn felt a little shy at first when she met the other women. For many years, she lived alone with her animals on her homestead. Millie had been one of her only friends, and they only saw each other every few months.

She needn't have worried. They welcomed her into their group. Blaze's mate Phoebe was homesteading like Falyn. Darken's mate Gina specialized in aerated concrete construction, while Stalker's mate Neely finished law enforcement training, becoming a protector. Vyken's wife, Danya, who was just showing pregnant, was an educator at the Enclave Learning center near new Chicago. Shadow Hawk and Falcon Rader had been matched from the genetic database of women hoping to find a cyborg mate. This gathering was the first time meeting them.

They shared how they met their mates on their first evening together. Jenna's and Alia's first sight meeting were tame compared to the others. Jenna was from New Chicago, and Shadow Hawk picked her up at her home and took her out to dinner. Falcon Rader met Alia in his territory, and they went sightseeing on his sky cycle and stopped to have a picnic.

It almost seemed like an elite club.

"The thing about these guys is that you never have to wonder where you stand with them. Their only fault is they are a little possessive, and the only time they get angry at you is if you carelessly put yourself in danger."

"Do you want to know something infuriating?" Phoebe asked. "When I get angry about something, he is so damn calm and reasonable."

They all laughed.

"There are no silly games or chasing other women. You know they love you and only you," said Danya. "You can all go on the matchmaking database from your com-tablets to tell other women considering applying for a cyborg match."

"I like having the freedom to do the things I love," Gina said. "I've helped build a lot of new houses."

"I'm learning how to fly," said Phoebe.

The conversation drifted away from being mated to cyborgs to the things those relationships freed them to do. They didn't have to live in a continued state of survival mode.

Each bride had a different style and color of dress for the occasion. Falyn's was a pale green mint color. The bodice was fitted with a partially gathered skirt that was long in the back and mid-thigh length in the front. Underneath, she wore a matching pair of leggings. Gina and Phoebe chose a similar style in pale yellow and pale blue. Neely and the others chose ankle-length dresses in lavender, pink, aqua, and a piece of shimmery fabric that combined pastel colors. Each outfit had matching sandals.

Each couple brought a dish to pass for the wedding meal. Starting the ceremony, the women came outdoors and down the steps with crowns of flowers in their hair. Danya led and joined Vyken under the trellis. The other women joined their mates in turn.

"Before we repeat our vows, I want you all to know I hold you in high esteem for your accomplishments in restoring law and order to the Enclave territories. I didn't want to return to a devastated Earth after all the years of war. The one thing that changed my mind was the possibility of finding Danya, my mate. I think that's why we all came back. It was not the empty promise we all thought. Our promised mates are here. Finding them was up to us. And, now, here we are."

"Repeat after me and fill in the proper name. I, Vyken Dark, take you, Danya Hill as my beloved lifelong mate. I will protect, honor, and care for you and any offspring we make. I am yours, and you are mine as long as I draw breath."

When the males finished, the women were led in the same vow by Danya. She pronounced them all husbands and wives and directed them to kiss their mates.

Their procession from the house and their brief ceremony was all recorded by bumblebee drones buzzing around, each couple repeating their vows.

They shared the meal they all prepared afterward, then each couple drifted off to consummate their marriage with love and great enthusiasm.

Epilogue

Before their group wedding, Max and Falyn had gone East to look at horses for Max to ride. He was only getting one for himself, but they looked at three to see which one he felt a connection with. They found his horse, a big black gelding draft horse with white on his face and white feathering on his legs.

It was love at first sight for cyborg and horse. Falyn thought he was a bit pricy, but they had taken weeks to find draft horses for sale. They did find a litter of puppies at the one farm. The owner called them mutts, but the mother was a good stock dog. Falyn was taken by a multicolored male with long hair.

"I hadn't had a dog since before my parents died," Falyn told him. "I really like this one." She held it up and rubbed its soft fur on her cheek."

Of course, Max couldn't resist the pleading look in her eyes. "Well, I never had a dog, but it could be interesting."

The farmer didn't want credits because they were worth nothing, so Max sourced a new battery for his solar collectors in exchange.

Two weeks later, the horse Max picked arrived. The custom saddle from the New Mexico territory arrived a few days after that. The horse came with the name Jarrod; since he answered to it, Max saw no need to change it.

Jarrod was easygoing, and the other horses accepted him into their herd. The gangers' horses were returned to them, but they had found a couple of skinny strays wandering that they rescued. One was a pregnant mare.

Since they decided to live in Falyn's house, Max claimed adjacent unoccupied. Part of it was wooded, and part was overgrown farmland where they could grow crops.

They made a trail through the woods to the additional fields and rode horseback a couple times a week to check on the crops. Other times, Max sent surveillance drones.

A year and a half after letting Colton Price go, they got a vid message from him with his wife and their new baby. That made Max glad he let them go because the female was clearly happy and loved. Even Colton seemed different, doting on his wife and child.

While Max yearned to have children of his own, he also realized he wasn't ready to share Falyn even with his own offspring. He didn't bring up the subject because they'd already agreed to discuss it when Falyn felt prepared. After all, she was the one who would carry the child in her own body.

It would be centuries before they used nurturing tanks like those used in manufacturing cyborgs to grow normal babies. Max never wanted Falyn to feel pressured to have a baby or babies.

A little over two years into their marriage, they were basking in the afterglow of lovemaking, still joined. Falyn was caressing him, and she said, "I think I'm ready now."

"To go again?" he asked, thinking he could fuck her again.

She giggled up at him, and he frowned, not seeing why that was funny. It wasn't unusual for them to do that.

"I'm sorry." She stroked his cheek and brushed back his hair. "I should have said what I meant. I'm ready to have your baby. I want to have your baby… maybe a couple or three."

The joy on Max's face was beautiful to see. Falyn loved that she could be the source of that joy. She loved him.

Her first pregnancy brought them fraternal twins, a girl, and a boy. Two years later, they had a girl and a boy a year and a half after that.

As Max held their final boy for the first time, he didn't regret fighting one day for the love he found with Falyn and their four beautiful children. It was so worth his sacrifice.

Bonus Epilogue

Colton got up from his seat on his front porch, drinking down the last swallow of coffee in his mug. The sunrise colors were fading as the sun rose above the mountains in the distance. Every day he thanked the Universe and whatever gods there might be that his ordeal was finally over.

His beautiful Tessa was sleeping in their bed blissfully exhausted from making love until the wee hours. She seemed almost unsatiable since she became pregnant, he was more than willing and able to satisfy her.

The cybernetic enhancements augmented his sexual prowess considerably. He didn't hate those parts of him anymore. Those changes gave him the power and strength to keep going until he could find Tessa. Her love gave him the incentive.

Psychogenic therapy had wipe out most of Tessa's memories of her time with Thrix. The medic thought her addiction to *seronome* could have augmented the treatment to make her forget most of it. Fortunately, none of it came back after detox.

Colton heard as soon as she got up from their bed. She was moving stealthily through the house to sneak up behind him and surprise him. He set down his cup on the porch railing and waited, smiling. They'd played this little game since they we're kids.

Back then, she could surprise him, but not since they made him a cyborg. Tessa was almost there when he pivoted and swept her into his arms, lifting her and twirling them in a circle.

Her laughter was a beautiful sound he feared he would never hear again. He set her on her feet still holding her, and she put her arms around his neck, looking up at him, and licking her full lips.

"I win," she said with a smile.

"How do you figure that? I caught you."

"I got what I wanted." She grinned.

"What do you have in mind?

For her answer, she pressed her mouth to his for a sweet slow kiss.

Colton hadn't noticed until the kiss ended that she was naked. At least not consciously. He was only wearing a pair of shorts on this warm, summer morning. It didn't matter. Their cabin was so far away from any other homestead, there had never been a road to the property. She could be naked if she wanted to be.

"I love you, Colton Price. Always have, always will." She said the words looking straight into his eyes.

"And I love you, always…. Forever."

Colton could still remember the past, but he didn't let it haunt him anymore because he could see the future in Tessa's eyes.

The End

About the Authors

Clarissa Lake grew up watching Star Trek and reading Marvel Comics. She attended science fiction and fantasy conventions, where she met many well-known science fiction authors and attended their readings and discussion panels. They included sci-fi greats Anne McCaffery, CJ Cherry, George RR Martin, Ben Bova, Timothy Zahn, Frederik Pohl, and Orson Scot Card.

While she loves sci-fi, she always thought there should be more romance, so she started writing it hot and steamy.

Christine Myers has been a science fiction fan since seeing the original "Day the Earth Stood Still" at age eight. Her favorite subgenre is science fiction romance with interstellar space travel and a bit of space opera. Among the most influential in her work are the Lazarus Long novels by Robert Heinlein, including "Time Enough for Love" and Marta Randall's "Journey." She loves Star

Trek, Firefly, Farscape, and Veteran Cosmic Rockers, the Moody Blues.

After spending years trying to get her work published by traditional publishers, she discovered KDP and became an Indie Author/Publisher. This means she does it all from writing to publishing.

BOOKS BY CHRISTINE MYERS/CLARISSA LAKE

THE ALEDAN SERIES
PSION MATES Prequel
The Aledan PSION
OLTARIN
SURVIVING ZEVUS MAR
PSION FACTOR
PSION'S CHILDREN
CALAN

CYBORG AWAKENING SERIES
CYBORG AWAKENINGS Prequel
VYKEN DARK

WITH CLARISSA LAKE
JOLT SOMBER
TALIA'S CYBORG
AXEL REX

CYBORG RANGER SERIES
BLAZE
DARKEN
STALKER
MAX

Visit her websites for more information and FREE books:

https://clarissalake.authors.zone/
http://christinemyers.authors.zone

Printed in Great Britain
by Amazon